OMEGA'S BURNING HEAT

Omegaverse MPREG Romances

Michael Levi

Copyright © 2022 Michael Levi

All rights reserved

The characters and events portrayed in this book are fictitious. Any similarity to real persons, living or dead, is coincidental and not intended by the author.

No part of this book may be reproduced, or stored in a retrieval system, or transmitted in any form or by any means, electronic, mechanical, photocopying, recording, or otherwise, without express written permission of the publisher.

ISBN: 9798443687179
Imprint: Independently published

1st edition

Cover design by: Michael Levi

CONTENTS

Title Page
Copyright
Omega for Obsessive Alpha 1
Chapter 1 3
Chapter 2 9
Chapter 3 14
Chapter 4 19
Chapter 5 24
Yel's Epilogue 29
Feran's Epilogue 34
Omega for Protective Alpha 37
Chapter 1 38
Chapter 2 43
Chapter 3 48
Chapter 4 53
Chapter 5 58
Chapter 6 63
Chapter 7 68
Chapter 8 73
Chapter 9 78
Chapter 10 83

Chapter 11	88
Chapter 12	95
Chapter 13	100
Chapter 14	105
Chapter 15	110
Chapter 16	115
Chapter 17	120
Chapter 18	125
Bren's Epilogue	130
Cogwyn's Epilogue	135
Omega for Jealous Alpha	139
Chapter 1	140
Chapter 2	145
Chapter 3	150
Chapter 4	155
Chapter 5	160
Chapter 6	165
Chapter 7	170
Chapter 8	175
Chapter 9	180
Chapter 10	185
Chapter 11	189
Chapter 12	194
Chapter 13	199
Chapter 14	204
Nefion's Epilogue	209
Palio's Epilogue	214
Teaser: Overwhelming the Omega	219

MPREG Series and More	221
About the Author	223

OMEGA FOR OBSESSIVE ALPHA

CHAPTER 1

Feran

I felt something sniffing me, like he was trying to smell me. I cracked open my eyes as I found someone standing right in front of me. It was a man, huge, older than me, and hot as balls. The moment my eyes set on him, it was like fireworks exploded in my head.

I wanted to rip his clothes off his body and see what he was like naked. I wanted to slide my tongue over his muscles, to feel him for the man he was, to grind my body against his, and to make sweet love with him. I was already drooling even though I didn't even notice that yet.

The guy who was in front of me was so close I could smell the minty odor coming out of his mouth. His eyes were emerald green, his hair messy and blond, some stubble on his chin.

His face was chiseled and followed hard lines, making me want to put my hand on it and feel it until he was smiling.

And I just noticed I was supposed to be falling to the floor.

I felt something holding me in place so that that didn't happen. It was his arm, wrapped around my torso. It was firm, showing off his confidence. I was still in the same room from before, which was behind the bar where I was drinking away my sorrows.

I just remembered something terrible that happened not too

long ago, which made me come running to this place. I supposed I should be thankful he was holding me like this so that I didn't fall and hurt myself, but the way he was smelling me was also frightening and annoying. I should be shoving him away from me as fast as possible and as hard as I could, but that was easier said than done.

I wasn't going to say that I was skinny. In fact, I was lean and I did work out, but I didn't follow any diet and I didn't inject my body with anything. This guy, on the other hand, looked more like a gym rat than anything.

And he was even more frightening because his body was covered in tattoos. There was even one of them, which caught my attention the most, sneaking from under his shirt and going across his neck.

It was the tattoo of a lone wolf, making me remember that he was probably from *that* MC gang. I shivered at the thought of having caught the attention of one of them. It was the worst thing that could be happening.

Not to mention that I didn't have anything to do with him...

He parted his lips, blowing a bigger cloud of his mouth's odor over my face. I closed my eyes and scrunched up my nose, but not because I was turned off by the smell, but because his scent was overwhelming.

As an Omega, I was always subjected to this kind of situation, especially when the other guy was an Alpha. And it wasn't just the smell coming out of his mouth that was making me hard and aroused right now. It was also his musky scent, which came from all around his body.

"I just saved you from hurting yourself. I think you should be thanking me." And as soon as he finished saying that, he smiled, showing me his perfect teeth. I always thought that bikers like him didn't brush their teeth, but it looked like he was an exception.

I knew he was a biker because of the patch he had on the

front of his leather jacket. It showed that he, indeed, was from one of the biker gangs in the region. They were called the Wolf Bikers, and everyone around here in the city feared them. They were a menace, robbing people and their houses, causing the police all sorts of troubles.

I knew that coming to this bar was a mistake, but I didn't think I was going to run into a member of the Wolf Bikers.

I shot my hands to his chest, shoving them against it. I thought he was going to leave me alone and add some distance between us, but he held his ground, tightening how hard his arm was pressing against my torso.

"Hey! Leave me alone!" I yelled, hoping that someone in the bar was going to hear me, but as time passed, I realized I was alone. I shouldn't even have come into this room to cry alone.

But when I was in the main room of the bar, some Alphas were bothering me. They couldn't keep their arousal in check when I stepped into the place, and thus they were hitting on me all the time. I grew annoyed and ended up stumbling into this room.

One curious thing about that was that this guy was not with them. Even though I was a little drunk, I was certain of that because those bikers were from a different gang. They were called the Bear Bikers, and they were even bigger of a problem than the Wolf Bikers.

"I don't think so, sunshine." His voice was low, throaty, almost like he was always grumpy. And yet, it was still sexy and very much like the kind of voice I liked in a man. "I know your family has a lot of money."

I locked my eyes with this, shivers running down my spine. The way he said that, it could only mean one thing.

I tried to shove him away from me again, only to find his strong and determined chest standing in my way once more. He didn't move, not even an inch. "I'm not going anywhere with you!"

He dipped his head, making me feel that his lips were going to connect to mine. And even though they were perfect lips that made me want to kiss him over and over, I wasn't going to fall for that.

I wasn't going to let my feelings for him get in the way of what I was supposed to do. I needed money for the operation, and I was going to get it, one way or the other.

I did remember something interesting and a little frightening, which I was trying not to think about. I sure as hell didn't want to think that it was true. My father once said that I was going to marry someone I was meant to be with. He said that I was fated to be his, that God wanted things to be that way.

I punched that thought out of my mind right away. My father said that when he was better and also when he was on his deathbed. It meant a lot to him that I married the right Alpha, which was one reason why I was willing to be with anyone who wanted something more long-term with me.

The only problem with that was that nobody wanted that. Everybody was always just looking for a quick fuck.

"I didn't say I was going to kidnap you, but now that you brought it up, I think I just might," he growled, bringing his arm up so that I was standing, and then pushing me forward until we were crossing the door out of the bar.

Moments later, my feet were crunching over the grass and my eyes were greeting the glow of the moon. I looked around, screaming out of my lungs as I hoped that someone was going to save me.

But no one was. We were in one of the most forgotten neighborhoods in the city, where not even the cops came here. I would be lucky if anyone even opened their window to find out what was going on.

His hand shot to my mouth, shutting it. He dipped his head until his lips were next to my left ear. "Stop yelling or I'm going to hurt you, and you really don't want to find out how much I can hurt."

Shivers ran down my spine again when I realized I was hearing something loud coming in our direction. Snapping my head to it, the first thought that came into my mind was that it was a cop, on a motorcycle, who witnessed what was happening.

I blinked twice, clearing up my vision, only to realize that it wasn't the police. It was just another biker, from the Bear Bikers gang.

He was on his motorcycle and was riding it like he was the king of the world. Pulling over, he pulled a pistol out of his leather jacket and pointed it at the kidnapper.

He pulled up the left corner of his lips before affirming, "Thanks for bringing him out, but this one is mine."

I crept my head around to glance at my kidnapper. Fur was beginning to grow on his face, his teeth becoming larger and pointy.

I already knew he was a wolf shifter, but I never thought he was going to transform right in front of me. He was already large and much bigger than me in his human form, and now the difference was becoming frightening. Much, much more. He made me feel tiny and unforgettable before him.

The Bear biker on the motorcycle cocked his gun, widening his smile. "You think you can survive a silver bullet to the heart? I'm not going to hold back on pulling the trigger, if I have to."

I thought the Wolf Biker was going to continue his transformation and fight against the other guy, but he did the opposite. Moving his arm away from me, he put his hand behind my back and shoved me forward, forcing me to stumble across the grassy field until I fell into the arms of the Bear Biker.

The latter wrapped one of his arms around me, revved up the motorcycle, and rode away after shoving me into the backseat while keeping his gun pointed to the wolf shifter.

Still drunk, the combination of everything happening with me was too overwhelming, and before long, I was closing my eyes and I couldn't reopen them.

    I passed out and I had no idea what was going to happen.

CHAPTER 2

Yel

I stomped hard onto the grass, my fangs growing bigger. Fisting my hand, I couldn't help but feel like punching that bear biker until blood was gushing out of his mouth. I was going to bash his head against the pavement until his skull cracked, I swore.

I couldn't believe I was so amateur about it. I should have realized someone was going to come after him, too. I was going to make bank by kidnapping Feran.

Stomping on the grass again, all I could do was turn back and stride over to Delight, my bike. It was parked in front of the bar.

The members of the Wolf Bikers didn't know that I was here. They didn't frequent this part of town. I was the only one here, and the only one who should have known about Feran.

He was from one of the most important families in the city. I knew that kidnapping him would make me a lot of money. I didn't even feel bad about it, and I wouldn't either way. The money his family would have to hand over wouldn't even dent their fortune, after all.

I couldn't lose this opportunity.

The moon high above the buildings and the houses, I looked up at it as I realized how easy it would have been to turn into a wolf while that Bear Biker was pointing his gun in my direction.

In a fair fight, did he think he would win?

Fuck that guy. He'd always been a nuisance. He was keeping tabs on me.

Ennith...

I was going to punch his gut so hard one day he would puke whatever was in his stomach, I swore, swinging my leg over Delight and remembering all the things that happened between us.

All the clashes we had, even when he was in school and trying to prove to the teachers he was better than me at pretty much anything. He joined up with the Bears because they were the right fit for him.

Turning on the engine of the motorcycle and propelling it forward, crossing one red traffic light after the other without even putting on my helmet, I was focused on just one thing – finding Ennith and Feran. I was pretty sure I knew where he was taking him to.

The Bear Bikers' hideout.

It wasn't too far and even though I wasn't going to have the support of the Wolf Bikers, I should be okay. I didn't need them, anyway. I was pretty confident in how well I could sneak in and out of that place. It was pretty big, with ample free space. I was going to have to keep my guard up all the time, but it wasn't a challenge impossible to tame.

I smirked, feeling overconfident. I had my gun with me now. I'd left it in the motorcycle because I didn't think I was going to have to use it during the kidnapping. I thought it was going to be simple.

Feran was pretty small, a little lean, weak, and very submissive. Me being the Alpha I was, he was always going to smell me and fall to his knees when his nose got a sniff of it. I mean, everything was going according to plan before Ennith popped up.

I couldn't help but feel aroused by Feran, though. He had short, dark hair, perfect lips, ocean-blue eyes, and lips that were just the right size.

When I enclosed my arm around his torso, the first thought that popped up in my mind was how much I wanted to rip the clothes off his body and bend him over. It only didn't happen because raping was something I would never do.

He was about 10 years younger than me, too. That was a piece of information I dug out on the internet. And that age gap was a plus for me, too.

If we had met under different circumstances, I'd be going for him for sure. The only problem with that was that now he thought of me just as an asshole who was trying to kidnap him.

Being the person I was, I couldn't care less about that.

I pulled up not too far from their hideout, pushing my motorcycle until it was hidden in a dark and forgotten alleyway between two massive buildings.

I pulled up my hood, shadowing my face, and went to one of the doors that two guards were by the side of.

Their hands went to their pistols as soon as they realized someone was padding over to them.

"Back off if you don't want to get hurt, jackass," one of them barked, pulling out his pistol when I swung my arm, striking him square on the side of his head. He fell limp on the floor, and I fished out his pistol before his partner could do anything. He stumbled backward, trying to pull the trigger of his pistol, but it was too late.

Yanking out my own pistol after storing the other I'd just snagged, I popped a bullet in his brain. The muffled sound caused by the silencer comforted me that nobody had heard anything. Smiling without showing my teeth, I searched their bodies until I found what I was looking for – the side door's key.

I opened it, snuck into the building, and then skulked down the hallways until I found the room I was looking for. After knocking out the guards protecting it, I crept open the door and found what I was looking for.

The Omega, strapped to a chair, still asleep. He was beaten up pretty badly. His face was covered in bruises and cuts, the region around his eyes bigger and swollen.

I felt a little bad for him, but not for longer than a couple of seconds. I went around him, sliced the rope on his wrists, and slapped his face so that he woke up. He flapped open his eyelids, snapping back to reality. "Wait, what?" He murmured, looking at me with dreamy eyes.

But then he panicked and started to struggle against the chair, almost toppling over. I yanked him to me before that happened and grabbed him with my arms, hugging him tightly.

"Woah there, little Omega. Not about to let you hurt yourself. After all, your family will pay less for you if that happens."

"I don't get it…" He murmured, closing his eyes all of a sudden and falling limp in my arms. I groaned, realizing that I was going to have to take him out of the building with me.

Sneaking through the guards had already been difficult without having to do that, and now it was going to be even harder.

I sighed, put him over my shoulders, and then went out of the room.

I skulked down the hallways, creaking open the door where I had come from. Inching my head outside, I turned my head left and right to see if anyone had come to see what happened here.

But I was so fast since entering the building that they hadn't had time to figure that out yet. The way ahead was clear, with no cars driving on the roads or pedestrians ambling on the sidewalks.

I smirked, closing the door behind me after remembering that I stored the bodies of those guys in a dumpster in the alleyway on the left. I placed Feran back on the ground, slapped his face until he reopened his eyes. He glanced me over, snapping his head from left to right as he tried to process what was happening.

The poor guy was still dazzled by the recent chain of events.

I put my arm around his shoulders, keeping him clutched to me as I took him to where I had left Delight.

And just when we were crossing the sidewalk to the next block, I heard a shot coming from behind me.

CHAPTER 3

Feran

The shot echoed in the darkness, blood spilling out and smearing my face. I screamed, but I couldn't run away. I was frozen in place as I saw that a biker was running toward us. He had a pistol in his hand and was pointing it at the kidnapper again.

His body fell against mine, and I almost lost my balance and toppled over on the road with him. Locking his eyes with me, he muttered, "Take me to Delight. It's there – in the alley between those two buildings. Be fast about it because, otherwise, we won't have enough time."

I snapped my head in the direction he was pointing with his finger, still feeling his body a little too heavy against mine. The Bear Biker, running toward us, was still a significant distance away, and if I hurried up, we could get there before it was too late.

Problem was, I didn't think that was wise, nor did I think I should do that. After all, why should I help the guy that was trying to kidnap me?

The truth was that I shouldn't, but I also didn't know how to drive his motorcycle and I would be helpless in this neighborhood. It wasn't just that Bear Biker that was coming for us.

It was now a whole battalion of them, all sporting pistols

and submachine guns. If I didn't hurry up and make a decision quickly, everything would be lost, and I and this guy would be locked up in the building again.

He slapped my face all of a sudden so hard it left a mark, my skin stinging. I had a choice of doing this on my own, most likely finding myself at the mercy of the Bear Bikers again, who probably had the same plans for me, or running away with this Wolf Biker, who was at least hurt.

I wasn't going to say that I had better chances of escaping if I chose the latter, but at least it made me feel hopeful.

It was like everything was happening in slow motion for me. Pushing my body forward, I dragged him across the sidewalk as we entered the alleyway. His motorcycle was parked there and nobody had seen it.

I peeked behind my shoulder and witnessed the Bear Bikers closing the distance. They were fast – faster than I thought they were, especially for guys so big who were already transforming.

Their fangs were popping out and their teeth were growing bigger, fur showing on their skin. Not too long from now, they were going to be not humans anymore, but bears, and I didn't want to stick around until then.

I took a deep breath, swinging my leg over the motorcycle and enclosing my arms around the torso of the biker. They had shot him in his belly, but the bullet had not gotten stuck inside of him.

Blood was still leaking through his clothes and I had no idea if he had enough energy to ride the bike back to where he lived. This was all a mess, which I could have prevented by not going to that bar in the first place.

The biker peeked over his shoulder, glancing at me. "Hang on tight. This is going to be a wild ride."

Hearing that, all I could do was what he wanted. Even though I felt disgusted that I needed him now, I pressed my head against his back and tightened up my arms around his torso. He twisted the handles of the motorcycle, propelling it forward and through the hoard of bikers running toward us.

More shots echoed in the darkness and all I could do was hope they weren't going to kill me or the biker trying to save himself. I could feel how strained and tense his body was, his skin growing warmer. I didn't like that, and it was making me worry he wasn't going to make it.

I closed my eyes tight until they were like slits, hearing the rumbling of the motorcycle's engine. The wind blowing against my face, I thought I wasn't going to make it too when I heard a bullet whizzing past my left ear. That was close. Too close.

My heart was pounding so hard I didn't even realize I was clutching on to my kidnapper, hoping that he was going to save me. I felt the motorcycle swerving, riding across the streets, and then going to a place that was underground.

The blowing wind was no more, the air around me growing colder all of a sudden. I cracked open my eyes, turning them left and right to figure out where I was. I couldn't even see the buildings and the houses that permeated the neighborhood where I had been. I couldn't even see the moon high in the sky anymore.

I was somewhere different, in a place underground like I thought before. I could see white fluorescent lights above our heads and pillars dotting the place. Turning my eyes left and right again, I could also see some cars and other motorcycles parked here.

We were in a parking lot under the building.

He peeked over his shoulder, glancing at me. Scrunching up his nose, I thought he was going to say something. For a moment, his eyes kept on looking at me and I had no idea how to react. It was the first time I was clutching on to a guy like this, feeling the hardness of his muscles under his leather jacket.

I moved away from him, getting off the bike as he tried to do the same. But as soon as his feet were on the ground, he lost his balance and fell over. Blood was still seeping out of his wound, and it looked like he wasn't going to make it.

I glanced around, hearing only the silence in the darkness of the parking lot.

I had the option of just running away and leaving him where he was, but then I saw that there were cameras in the parking lot.

Whether or not they were working, I couldn't know for sure right now. That meant if I ran away, the police would know I was involved in his death. Glancing down at him, I could see the pain in his face and that his eyes were losing their light.

He glanced at me, smiling as if he was mocking me – as if he knew what I was thinking.

"Take me to my room and I can erase every recording those cameras are making right now."

"Right, and then you'll lock me up and force my family to pay the ransom." I sighed, stepping away from him. "I can't do that. I don't want to put my family at risk."

He exhaled, pressing his hand against his wound. When he glanced back at me, he proposed, "Let's cut a deal. You will take me to my room, will help me get better, and then I'll let you go."

"How can I know you aren't lying? I don't trust you." I took another step away from him and was almost ready to get out of this place.

He pushed himself up until he was sitting on the floor. Even though he was smiling without showing his teeth, I could tell that the pain was eating him up from the inside. His face was paler than before.

"I'm giving you my word. You know that, as an Alpha, that means a lot to me."

He was right, but that still wasn't enough. What was, however, forcing me to help him was those damned cameras who were probably still recording this. I knew what the police were like in the city.

They would probably lock me up before even asking what happened and why I was involved in his death.

I felt a pang of pain when I realized how bad I would feel if I left him alone in this parking lot. I supposed I could call an ambulance, but then I'd have to give them my personal information, and I didn't want to take that risk.

No to mention that it would take them forever to get here. By the time the ambulance arrived, it would be too late for this Alpha whose name I didn't even know.

I shook my head, padding over to him as I grabbed his hand and helped him up. Chances were I was making the wrong decision, but from the looks of it, as long as he didn't die, I should still have enough time and a good opportunity to escape.

I couldn't believe I was helping my kidnapper, though.

CHAPTER 4

Yel

I cracked open my eyes, realizing that Feran was sleeping on the chair where he was sitting the night before. He didn't need to take the bullet out of my body. It sliced straight through the flesh, and it didn't hit any of my organs.

It just hurt like hell. And I supposed I should be thankful that this guy decided to help me even though the cameras in the parking lot had stopped working a long time ago. I wouldn't be living here if it had so much surveillance.

I sat on the bed, sniffing his scent. He smelled me too, which was one of the reasons I noticed he was hard that moment we met up at the bar. I was surprised he even decided to stay. I thought he was just going to leave me alone in the room.

I checked him out, from bottom to top, feeling a little bad that he spent so much effort healing me – going as far as dressing my wound – and I didn't do anything to help him, other than getting him out of the Bears' hideout, that was.

Everything was so quiet in the room and around the apartment building that someone would hear a pin falling to the floor. I was already feeling better, even though I could still feel some pangs of pain coming from where the bullet hit me.

Fucking Ennith. He always had to ruin everything and was always keeping tabs on me. Well, now he couldn't know where we were. I just moved into this project, and it would take the Bear Bikers and other gangs weeks before finding out about it.

If there was something the landlord prided himself in, it was that he kept everyone's secrets hidden and never ratted anyone out.

I thought that the Bear Bikers would have managed to chase me on their bikes, and even though I was pretty sure they tried, I didn't hear any of them getting anywhere near here.

The police weren't going to look too deep into what happened, and those filthy assholes that Ennith lived with weren't going to be much of a bother. That meant I should be safe.

I was an asshole. I'd admit that any day and I'd never lie about it, but I also... couldn't say that I didn't feel sorry for him. He shouldn't even be involved in this, and he wouldn't be so hurt now without my showing up in his life.

I got off the bed and nudged his shoulder, waking him up. He was a rich asshole who thought he was better than everyone, just like the rest of his family, but I wasn't heartless. His wounds needed to be dressed, and that's what I was going to do.

I wondered what would happen if he knew something that was once told to me a long time ago.

Feran cracked open his eyes, staring at me wide-eyed. He jumped off the chair where he was sitting, scooting away from me. I held up a hand so that he knew I wasn't going to hurt him.

The truth was, I had a softer heart than most people thought I had.

"Stay away from me!" He shouted, picking up a chair and brandishing it at me. "I made a mistake. I shouldn't have helped you. I should have run away when I had the chance."

I lowered my hand. "Does it look like I'm going to hurt you?" I queried, sighing. This was going to be a pain in the ass if he didn't give me another chance. "Plus, I've already changed my mind."

He lowered the chair, but didn't let go of it. Widening his

eyes, he said, "What do you mean? I don't trust you."

I could smell his scent. It was perceivable, but not as strong as an Alpha's, as it wasn't supposed to be. I couldn't help but feel aroused by the way he was so scared of me, his pinkish lips, his rosy cheeks, and his jet-black hair. He was cute and my type.

"If I wanted to rope you to a chair, I'd already have done that." I locked my eyes with his, hoping that it was going to be enough to convince him.

He opened his hands, letting go of the chair. I proceeded to him, measuring the weight of my steps. Now that we were closer to where I wanted to be with him, I wanted to give ourselves a chance.

I could have at least a one-night stand with him, right? Just to wipe away the terrible thing I did today, and to thank him for dressing my wound...

"I suppose you're right," he murmured more to himself than to me, rounding the chair and sitting on it. I cracked open a gentle smile as I proceeded to him, grabbed everything I was going to need, and started to dress up his wounds.

Minutes later, when I was almost finished with that, I looked up at him. His eyes were avoiding mine, most likely wishing he didn't have anything to do with me.

"I'm sorry this had to happen to you."

"Now you are feeling sorry about it? My family is probably worried sick about me."

"I've got my phone with me. If you want to call them, you can."

Feran didn't say anything for the next few minutes, waiting until I was finished. I patted him on the shoulder when I finished dressing up the wound there. He looked to the left, muttering, "Thanks."

And it was at that moment, when his eyes went back to looking at me and I was holding his gaze, that our lips connected.

I was kissing the most handsome Omega I'd seen in my life,

and it was washing away all the memories that came with me kidnapping him. I should never have done that.

My lips pressing and rubbing against his, I was taken by the strength of this moment and I couldn't think about anything else.

I drove my tongue into his mouth, put a hand on his waist, and pulled him up. I forced him to moonwalk until his back was bumping against the wall, a cloud of air escaping his mouth.

I thought he was going to protest and push me away from him, but Feran was actually immersing himself in the kiss. He was melting against me, and I was pressing my body harder against his. My hands roaming over his body, I couldn't help but start to pull up his shirt.

When I was mere moments from finishing that, he shoved his hand against my chest and made me scramble away from him. Feran was gasping for air when he asked, "What the hell was that?"

I smirked, settling both of my hands on the wall behind him. My face was so close to his we could kiss again and he wouldn't be able to do anything about it.

"Something I should've done a long time ago," I muttered, crashing my lips against his lips one more time and yanking his shirt off of him. His chest was finally bare before my eyes, my hands already going for it and groping it as I felt how smooth his skin was.

I didn't tell him this before, but he was my promised Omega. My father told me so before he died. I had always known that, and the whole kidnapping thing was just a ruse. Looking into his eyes, I could tell that Feran thought the same thing. He could almost read what I was thinking.

Our tongues battled inside our months, and I had control of the kiss soon after. I was overwhelming him, my hands groping him and sliding to where his nipples were. I pinched one of them, drawing out a profound moan from his throat.

I wasn't satisfied with that and thus decided to pinch his other nipple. He moaned again, squirming against my arms. His hands worked to yank off my belt, which he managed to do. I heard it fall to the floor moments later, my cock harder than it had ever been.

I couldn't believe that I was finally claiming my promised Omega, something I thought would never happen. My father said he was the one I had always been looking for, but for many years I didn't believe him, not until the moment when I met him in person for the first time.

His hands moved to my pair of boxer briefs, lowering it as he pushed it down. I stepped out of them, grabbing my dick and pointing it toward him.

He looked down, already getting to his knees. I could feel the hunger and thirst in his eyes, and also fear and desperation. I could tell it was the first time he was doing this, having sex with another man, and even though he was afraid, he was going on.

I was going to make this morning unforgettable for him.

CHAPTER 5

Feran

Light streaks snuck into the room, providing enough illumination so that I could make out what was happening. I was on my knees in front of a strong and overconfident Alpha, who had been in this kind of moment many times in his past. He was stroking his massive, impressive dong, and everything had been such a whirlwind I couldn't help but feel that this wasn't even the weirdest thing I did today.

The weirdest would definitely be saving this man's life just so that we could be doing this. I mean, I never planned for it.

He stroked my cheek and I lowered my head when he said, "You're my fated mate. You wouldn't be doing this if you weren't."

And he was right. While this was happening all of a sudden and it didn't make sense that it was, this man was the person I'd always been looking for all of my life. His musky scent told me so. The fact he dressed my wounds even though he didn't need to showed me the same.

One more thing made me believe that too, and it was the fact that I was getting wet for him. This wouldn't be happening if he wasn't my fated Alpha. I never felt so wet and hard for someone before, the thought of bending over and parting my legs for him permeating my mind…

"I know," I murmured, remembering how crazy this whole thing was. One moment I was willing to kill him, the next he was dressing up my wounds, and now we were making love.

My hands were shaking. I didn't know what I was supposed to do. This being my first time, I felt like I was walking on eggshells. One wrong thing I did and I'd feel like I disappointed him, which was something I could never do to my promised Alpha.

The one.

My fated mate.

My heart pounding in my head, I wrapped my lips around his bulbous cockhead and worked it with my tongue, focusing on the lower region just under the tip. That's where he was most vulnerable and how I was going to win him over.

My other hand worked his balls as I noticed how low they hung. I played with them, wondering if he was thinking the same thing. Was he going to get me pregnant? I didn't know, but it was just something we – fated Alphas and Omegas – did, and it was like it was calling to me.

And the worst thing about this was that I didn't even know his name.

I didn't even realize he was moving until he was sitting down on the bed. Still with my mouth on his cock, I kept on swirling my tongue around his bulbous cockhead, tasting the pre-come that was coming out through the slit. It was salty and delicious.

My eyes were closed as I continued to work on his balls with my hand, my other hand roaming over his thigh as I felt his muscles and how hard they were.

I could do this for hours on end, if only I didn't have something else more important to do, but which I was keeping locked behind a closed door.

It wasn't long until his balls were hotter than they had ever been, his shaft throbbing in my mouth. My hand went over his thigh and then his abs, groping that part of him, which was so perfect. His muscles were hard and I just wanted to be feeling them with my hands for hours on end.

He moaned, throwing his head back as he felt, now stronger than ever before, that he was close to his orgasm. Bobbing up and down on his cock, his hands massaged my shoulders and kneaded my skin.

Pulling my hand back from his balls, I started to stroke my own dick fast, my hand shooting up and down in a blur. I was close to reaching my climax as well, but I was only going to do that when he was inside of me.

I pulled my head back, glancing down at his cock. His shaft was still mighty and hard, pre-come seeping out of the slit. I collected saliva in my mouth, letting it drool over his dick. He was all lubed up and ready to penetrate me.

My hole was already clenching at the thought of that happening.

I climbed up on him, inching my head to his. I could feel his hot breath on my face as I murmured, "Breed me. Knot with me. Make me yours."

He let out a hot cloud of air through his nostrils, grabbing my shoulders and spinning me around until I was lying down in the bed. He climbed up on top of me, pressing his lips against me one more time. His hands groped me and roamed over my body, kneading my skin.

"I'm going to do everything I can to make you happy," he promised, showing me that all the things he had been feeling for me this whole time were true. My suspicions were right.

I shuddered under his might, wishing he was already inside of me. I couldn't help but wish I already knew his name, but that was something for later.

He grabbed my thighs, shoved my legs over his shoulders, and then, in one fell swoop, impaled me. I felt his impressive cock breaching through every barrier my hole had. He barged through them like they were made of nothing.

In less than a fraction of a second, he was all the way inside of me, and I was holding his gaze for what felt like an eternity.

I tried to control my breathing, but it was almost impossible. My body was growing hotter as the seconds passed, and I could already tell this was going to be so painful I was going to be screaming through the whole thing.

The Alpha bent his body until his head was right above mine, teasing me for another kiss.

He parted his lips and asked, "How are you feeling?"

I closed my eyes, urging him to go on. "Better than ever, and I just want you to knot with me. Breed me."

Hearing that, he widened his smile and started to move in and out of me, his pace slow and controlled in the beginning. I matched him thrust for thrust, knowing that I was making the best choice of my life.

Yes, nothing of this made any sense, but it still felt right. I felt a strong and compulsive connection to this mighty Alpha because he was my fated mate.

His fur started to grow over his body, his teeth becoming pointed and bigger. The Alpha was reaching his orgasm and I knew that, when he was there, nothing would hold him back.

His massive cock grew even larger inside of me, knotting me like I'd begged of him. He peppered my neck with several kisses, and then picked up his pace when he felt he was closer. His balls slapping against my butt, I couldn't help but immerse myself in a world of dreams when my orgasm swept through my body like a tsunami.

I was gasping for air when the Alpha started to pump out his hot, thick load, coating my walls with it. It was perfect.

He was knotting me and breeding me, and I couldn't help but imagine what our child would look like. So many things to mull over, my family and other people getting worried sick about me, and that was the first thought popping up in my mind.

Truth was, it was the overwhelming joy and connection I felt to him that confirmed all of my suspicions. I was mating with my promised Alpha…

His shaft gave a couple of last spurts before beginning to lose shape and size. The Alpha pulled out, plopping on the bed and wrapping his arm around me. I pressed my lips to his, immersing myself in his strong and confident arms.

His body was as sweatier as mine was and we soaked the bedsheets wet. Moments later, I couldn't contain the rising urge surging in my mind, and I had to ask him an important question.

But just when I parted my lips to do so, he murmured, "I'm Yel."

And then it was when everything became clear to me.

YEL'S EPILOGUE

I pulled up the motorcycle, stopping in the parking lot by the hospital. Since that moment at the bar when everything happened, the last thing I thought would happen was me falling in love with him. But it was a different matter altogether when I found out he was my promised Omega.

He got off the bike, grabbing my hand when I pulled him by the scruff of his neck as I crashed my lips against his one more time. My father had always told me I was going to find my promised Omega, and I never believed him.

I never believed him until I looked at this man's eyes and I felt a strong, impulsive bond with him. It was then I knew he was the one.

And to think I had once planned on kidnapping him... I was out of my mind then.

He pulled his head back, and I grabbed his hand and squeezed it.

"Are you sure you don't want me to go there with you?" I asked, getting off the bike. It didn't matter what he said and what his answer was going to be. I was going to be nearby, even if I couldn't be right there on the same floor with him.

He shook his head, smiling gently and looking so cute he made me want to kiss him again.

"Don't worry about it. I'm going to be fine, really. I'm just going up there."

I sighed, settling my hands on his love handles as I neared my head to his one more time. I was smelling his scent, how it was calling to me, and how it made me want him more and more.

"You know I can't help but worry about you. I wasn't always looking for you, but now that I know we are meant to be together, I want to be with you all the time."

"I know," he murmured into my mouth, brushing his lips over mine for a fraction of a second. His hand moving down over my shoulders, I knew that this was the moment to part ways with him, even though it was only going to take a couple of hours. Those were going to be hours that were going to feel like an eternity to me, but that was okay. I could wait.

He turned around, padding over to the door of the elevator. I sighed, crossing my arms over my chest as I raked him with my eyes. I checked him out from bottom to top as I wished I was yanking off his clothes and making love with him one more time in our bed.

I turned off the motorcycle, went over to the wall by the elevator after it was already taking him to the floor where his father was, and leaned against the wall. I remembered when I was in the same situation he was. Losing one's father was never a good thing, especially when we needed their help the most.

I couldn't go up there because he was going to say his goodbyes to his father. I didn't like thinking about it, but it was true. His father couldn't go on the way he was, and he wasn't going to make it. He was going to say goodbye to him.

It was like time was passing by with the speed of a thunderbolt around me, and I reopened my eyes when I felt a scent I knew too well. My body grew tense all of a sudden, tensing up my shoulders.

I heard his motorcycle coming over, pulling up in the parking lot. My body was burning with the heat of a furnace, my fangs sprouting out. I was growing larger, approaching him.

I wasn't going to let Ennith ruin this. He wasn't going to.

I marched up to him, stopping right in front of him. His fangs were coming out too, fur growing on his body.

"Get out of my way," he growled, pushing me with his hand. I was doing everything in my power not to start a fight at the hospital. I didn't want to cause a scene.

"I'm not going anywhere," I barked, my jacket and shirt tearing up to pieces. My body was growing larger, begging me to get on all fours because it knew that the other side of me was coming out. When it was out, I couldn't control it, and I'd run rampant in the city. I couldn't let that happen. It wasn't going to.

His eyes assumed the shape and the color similar to those of a bear, his canines bigger as his body was now covered by his thick and brown fur. In a battle against a bear, I didn't know who would win, but I wasn't going to hold anything back.

"You don't want this fight to happen," he growled again, swinging his leg as he hit me and made me fall over on my side. I kicked him with the sole of my boot, right where his belly was. He reached for it, snarling at me.

"That was good, but it's not going to stop me." Ennith dashed toward me, bringing his elbow down with all of his strength. If I hadn't jumped out of the way, he'd have hit me and cracked open my skull.

I growled, howling when I lunged at him. I was already becoming more monster-like, my pants ripping to pieces as spits of my saliva flew in different directions. I climbed up on Ennith, roaring as just one thought permeated my mind like nothing before it did.

I knew what Ennith had come here for – or rather, *who*. He also wanted Feran. Wanted him for himself and to steal him from me, but only over my dead body.

I kicked him away from me with the sole of my boot, clocking him in the face as he lost his balance. Ennith fell over with a loud thud, his body already enormous and growing bigger still.

His head's shape shifted, changed, and I could tell he was no longer human.

Now, more than anything, he was a bear, and he was going to fight me like one. His nails were bigger and sharper, and he sliced the air with them as he cut my cheek. Pain surged in my body and spread to every part of me, making my eyes look red and blood-filled.

Ennith hurt me, and it only made me want to kill him more than I already did.

He jumped back up, bolting toward me as I readied myself and sharpened my fangs. I was going for his jugular, and nothing was going to stop me.

I stopped in my tracks when I heard the ding of the elevator, the doors sliding open. Out of it stepped Feran, widening his eyes when he noticed what was happening. It was a surprise to him that I was already in my semi-transformed form and fighting against someone he knew well. The bastard in front of me was the one who hurt him to the point of knocking him out cold.

Ennith leaped at me, pulling up his arm as he pointed his fangs toward my neck. I brought my arm up, ready to block it and slice his neck with my own fangs when we heard the cops' wailing sirens. They poured into the parking lot, pulling up.

Seeing that, Ennith reversed his transformation and got back on his motorcycle. There was an entrance that was still not blocked by the police cars, which he burst through on his motorcycle. I stood where I was, gaping at him as he disappeared into the darkness of the city.

I reversed my transformation, my body going back to its human shape. I turned around, finding out that my Omega was running toward me.

He swung his arms around and buried his head on my chest, blurting out, "I had no idea he was going to come. I should've let you go up there with me."

I was naked like when I was born, feeling a little uncomfortable with all the cops surrounding us. They were going to have many questions for me, and I had no idea if I was going to have all the answers they wanted. All I knew was that I was back with Feran, who was still so special to me I kissed him again.

"Don't worry about it. I'm sure he won't be back. I'm going to make sure of it."

He softened up his eyes, tightening up our hug as he buried his head on my chest again. My heart slowing down, I could already feel much better than I was before. I could even pretend that the cops weren't around me, pointing their guns at us. They were afraid of the Alpha I was and what I could do.

People had always told me I was bigger and stronger than most other Alphas, which wasn't too far from the truth.

I kissed my Omega again and I knew that everything, from now on, was going to be much better.

FERAN'S EPILOGUE

I thought my father was going to have much more time than he did, but it wasn't meant to be. I was in front of his gravestone, hiding my tears as I felt the strong hands of my Alpha on me.

He had his hands on my shoulders, and he had been with me here for hours already. He didn't mention anything about that, but I still knew that it had already been hours since we came here.

"I'm sure he's proud of you," he murmured into my ear. My hand was roaming over my belly, which was now bigger than it had ever been. I was pregnant with Yel's baby and it was the most amazing moment in my life.

I took a deep breath in, turning around and burying my head on his chest just like it happened that one time he fought Ennith in the hospital's parking lot.

His arms were strong and as warm as they were then, bringing me the comfort and the support I was looking for.

I tilted my head up, gazing at his eyes. They were filled with his sense of understanding of what I was going through right now.

"It's over," he murmured, wrapping his arms around me and pulling me to him. "It's over and everything is going to be much better from now on."

I could feel his scent, his perfume, and how much he loved

me.

"But I still feel like it's never going to be over. I feel like there's always something pulling me back."

"It's over like it is between me and Ennith. He'll never get out of that prison."

He was right about that. His sworn nemesis was locked up soon after that attack in the parking lot, and now there was no chance he could ever be released. I felt safe as long as he was in prison.

He moved his arm up, putting it over my shoulders as he took me away from my father's gravestone. We were soon out of the cemetery, and I turned so that I was facing him. He put his hands on my cheeks, kissing me one more time.

I felt that the kiss lasted for hours, when in reality it lasted just a handful of seconds.

He looked into my eyes, making the same question from before, "Everything's better now, don't you think?"

I nodded, not forgetting about my father's death, but remembering the good memories I had with him. He was always going to be in my mind, no matter what happened.

We strolled across the sidewalk to the parking space by the cemetery. He got on his bike, put on his helmet – which was something he didn't use to do before meeting me – and then revved up the motorcycle. He looked behind his shoulder, asking, "Want to go for a ride with me?"

I nodded again, burying my head in the crook of his neck. I was always ready for a ride with him on his bike, and it was something that would never change. Not to mention that today was far too bright and colorful for me to be depressed over my father's death. He was one of the most important people in my life and he was always going to be.

But now it was time for my life to take the next step and start anew. Settling my head in the crook of his neck, I felt his beating heart and how comforting it was.

He revved up the motorcycle again, riding off seconds after. I was riding through the city with him and it was the most amazing thing in the world. I could feel the wind blowing against my face and I didn't want this moment to ever end, no matter what happened.

I was with my fated Alpha and everything was going to be splendid from now on.

OMEGA FOR PROTECTIVE ALPHA

CHAPTER 1

Bren

My heart was pounding harder than it had ever been. I was in a big room with my father, who was determined to show me that he'd found me my fated mate.

I couldn't believe that, after all this time, he still thought that way about it. I mean, when was the last time we had a marriage where someone was supposed to marry a certain someone else?

I was pacing back and forth in the room, my hand on my chin as I thought about all the possibilities. I wanted to consider all the possibilities which involved me getting out of this unharmed. I sighed, realizing that I was in trouble deeper than I thought.

I stopped in front of a ball by one of the sides of the room. I looked around me as I took in the fact that it was in a special place.

It was like a small house in the room and it was big enough just to house the sphere. I almost put my hand on it, but I didn't do it. I knew that it would have been wrong and that my father wouldn't have liked it.

I jumped when I felt something setting on my shoulder. I snapped my head around, looking over it. It was my father who was behind me and he was looking at the sphere on the pillar in the house, happiness and comfort in his eyes.

It was like he was telling me he was accomplishing something he had been dreaming about for a very long time.

"When you both put your hands on it, hopefully it'll tell me that you were indeed made for each other, just like the foreseer told me. He's never been wrong in his life."

My father was an Alpha and even though he had a strong scent, I couldn't feel it. Not the way I could feel other Alphas' scents, though.

He was tall and imposing, and I could tell why my other father married him. They were matched together just like it was happening to me now. They went to the foreseer and he told them that they were fated mates.

Back in his time, that was normal and expected of them, but nowadays I loved someone else and I sure as hell wasn't going to marry a biker.

He also came from a very powerful and influential family in the city, but he was different. He was rough, aggressive, and always thought so highly of himself. He was the opposite of me.

How could my father even think that we were going to be a good match?

"When I put my hand there and it tells me that I'm supposed to marry Ish instead, then what? Will you lock me up until you can change what the sphere says?" I asked, realizing I might be making a mistake. After all, my dad was just looking out for what was best for me.

He narrowed his eyes slightly, taking his hand off my shoulder. "Cogwyn should be here any second now." He stepped away from me and went to the door out of the room.

It was a room in a church, and from here we could see the street outside. I couldn't see any cars or motorcycles driving on the road or pedestrians on the sidewalks. We were alone here, almost like the world was trying to tell me that it had moved on from this kind of custom.

I went to the door with my father and I stopped in my tracks when I heard the rumbling of a motorcycle as it pulled over.

It was Cogwyn, riding his motorcycle without a helmet on. He put his right foot on the ground, swung his leg over the motorcycle, and then turned so that he was looking at me.

I spoke with him maybe once in my life and I wasn't looking forward to this. He was the kind of guy who just didn't make sense to me. He was rich and could become a CEO, and yet he was doing this. He decided to become a biker to get one up on his father, who was very similar to my dad. He also believed in fated mates.

I shook my head, whirled around, and then went to where the small house was in the church. I had no idea why it even was in the church of all places it could be. All I knew was that it was making me hate this whole thing more than I already did.

"What do you think you're doing?" My father asked, making a beeline to me.

"Getting this over with as soon as possible. This thing here is probably broken anyway. Regardless of what it tells me, I'm not going to marry that asshole."

My father put both of his hands on my shoulders, staring into my eyes. He was making me feel uncomfortable and he knew that.

"You are going to follow our tradition and carry it on. Don't disappoint me on this, Bren. Your Omega father probably thinks the same way."

I opened my mouth to rebuke him, only to realize that a certain scent was impregnating the room in the church. I was in front of the small house where the sphere was when I realized it was the Alpha's scent I was feeling. It was strong, thick, and it was like it was making it very hard for me to breathe.

I went to the side just to see him stepping into the church, a devilish smile on his face. As an Omega who had turned 18 not too long ago, I was horny most of the time, and I couldn't even control it. I couldn't even try to control it because it was just something that my body did.

I closed my nose with my hand, earning a scoff from Cogwyn.

He just walked past me and then went to the sphere, looking down with disdain at it.

"So, you're telling me that this thing will prove I'm supposed to marry this piglet?" He asked, disdain in his voice.

My father wasn't one to let anyone impose themselves and make fun of me and of his traditions, so he strode toward the biker and put himself right in front of him, staring at his eyes as he showed how determined he was about doing this.

"Any reason why your father didn't come here as well? He should have come here with you by now."

Cogwyn stared back at my father, not saying or doing anything. It was like sparkles of electricity were flying between their eyes. I knew that my father didn't look at Cogwyn with good eyes, but he still believed in the tradition more than any other person in the city did.

I guess I got lucky and unlucky at the same time. Things could certainly be worse right now if I was part of another family.

"He should be coming here soon," Cogwyn growled, stepping away from my father and then to the sphere in the small house.

He was lifting his hand when my father warned, "You can't touch it until your father is also here with us. You need to follow traditions like everyone else."

"Like everyone else? Nobody even does this anymore..." I heard him mumbling to himself, showing me that he was tough and brave, but not against my father. In a fair fight, I knew that he would beat him easily. He would wipe the floor with him.

I stepped toward them and was lifting my hand to get their attention when I realized a limousine was pulling over. I snapped my head toward it, realizing that it was Cogwyn's dad who was coming.

One of the guards opened the door of the limousine for him and he stepped out of it, adjusting his tie. Guards surrounded him as he walked into the church. He stopped by my father, who shook his hand.

"Parth, it's so good to see you again, my friend. I've been waiting for this moment since the foreseer told us about it."

"Same here. And first things first, we need to follow the first step. This won't happen the way we want unless we do it."

Misk chuckled, putting a hand on my father's shoulder as they went to the small house. They stopped in front of the sphere on the pillar and started to mumble about something. I was a bit lost about what was happening, being someone who didn't care about these traditions at all.

I turned my head left, realizing that Cogwyn wasn't even paying attention to what our fathers were doing. He was leaning against one of the walls, arms crossed over his chest.

It was now, just like so many other times I was with him, that I couldn't help but notice the tattoos on his arms. They almost covered the entirety of them and that, coupled with his short hair, determined eyes, and a beard to be made, made him look like a thug.

I shivered, thinking that our parents were planning on making us live together for the rest of our lives.

CHAPTER 2

Cogwyn

Why I was wasting time with this was beyond me. I supposed it was because I respected my father way too much and he didn't respect what I wanted. I uncrossed my arms from my chest when it looked like this was finally ending.

"So, can I finally put my hands on the sphere?" I asked, pretending that my 'fated' Omega wasn't by my side. He had a scent, but it wasn't strong and I could ignore it easily. That's what I was doing. Bren tsked, crossing his arms over his chest as he looked away.

Good, I thought. I liked him better when he showed me he didn't like me at all.

Parth turned his eyes to look at me and I felt conflicted feelings coming from him. It was obvious that he didn't like me as a person. After all, I was a biker and a member of the 1%. I was never going to be a good guy.

Nevertheless, he believed in the traditions and in what the foreseer told him that day.

"Yes, now it's time," he answered as he stepped away with my father. I studied his face as I hoped he was going to change his mind and tell me that we didn't have to do this.

But that wasn't going to happen and the Omega was already

standing by my side, in front of the sphere. It was glowing like it was calling for us.

I tsked, saying, "I just get this over with before I break it."

Bren didn't look at me, putting his right hand on the sphere as I put my left hand on it. It was warm, which was weird. I had no idea if the sphere was supposed to be this hot.

It glowed brighter all of a sudden, the light drawing me to it and making me feel like I was in a dream. Moments later, it dimmed and returned to its normal state. The temperature of the sphere dropped and I knew that soon it was going to say what it thought of us.

I moved my hand away from the sphere, stepping away from it. It wasn't that it scared me, but that I already knew I wasn't going to like the answer it had for us. Our parents stepped closer to the sphere, their eyes glowing in expectation.

This was incredibly important to them.

"Bren and Cogwyn-" the sphere was saying when a shot echoed in the room, hitting Bren's father right in his eye. I saw the hole that it made there, his body falling limp on the floor. Bren screamed and I felt sorry for him for the first time in my life.

A round of shots came from one of the windows, catching my father off-guard. He was running toward me when he fell over the floor, his body not moving anymore. Pain wrenched my heart as I realized I didn't know what I should be doing.

Bikers from the Bear Bikers' gang were storming the church, pointing their weapons at us. Bren yelled for his father to wake up as he rushed over to him, but a shot to the ground, right in front of his right foot, stopped him in his tracks.

My hand shot to my gun and I pulled it out. I aimed it and shot at the first guy I could see, a Bear Biker with a smug on his face.

He fell to the floor as his hand grabbed at his chest. His hand looked for his submachine gun, but I was already shooting at him in his head before he could do anything.

I grabbed Bren's hand and tugged at it when I realized that he was holding his ground. Snapping my head to him, I barked, "Do you want to die here with everyone or come with me? They're attacking us and they won't stop coming."

"I'm not leaving my father behind!" He argued, making me feel a little sorry for him. A tear was rolling down his cheek and I knew that he wanted to make sure his father was okay, but it was too late for that.

He should be thankful that he didn't die slowly. He got shot to his eye. I didn't think he even realized what was happening.

I aimed my pistol and shot at another biker in his head, his body falling through the window and then plopping on the floor. I yanked the little Omega to me with all of my strength, hurting him. I pulled him up so that he was looking straight into my eyes.

"I don't think I need to explain the situation to you, or do I?" I growled, my canines growing bigger as my nose felt all kinds of strong scents around us. Most of them were Alphas.

If they turned now, I wouldn't be able to fight against them. We wouldn't come out of this alive and this little Omega knew that very well.

He was cute, with round and rosy cheeks, but I didn't have time to sweeten my words. I had to shoot another biker that was storming into the church and hid behind the pillar, the Sphere of Revelations exploding into a million pieces right above our heads.

Bren screamed and I covered his mouth with my hand. I looked into his eyes as he studied my face. "Look, we're getting out of here and I'm going to take you home. I promise you that."

"But-"

"No buts. We need to get out of here before more of them come and this escalates. We don't have a lot of time." I felt the smoothness and the softness of his hand, wondering what it would be like if-

I shook my head, deciding not to think about that right now. It wouldn't do me any good.

I popped over the pillar, shot at a handful more of bikers, and then studied the room in the church. Spotting an exit, I jumped with the Omega and then leaped through the window, rolling outside with him. I was still gripping his hand tightly, and I wasn't going to let go of it.

The truth was that I cared about him, even if only at this moment. I knew what those Bear Bikers were looking for or, rather, who.

If and when they had their grubby hands on this Omega, they would do unspeakable things to him. I was part of the 1% just like them, but there were still things I'd never do.

"Let's go!" I shouted, tugging Bren with me as we sped over to Desire. My motorcycle was parked in an alleyway, hidden from everyone's eyes.

We heard speeding footsteps behind us, and I popped two shots at them. I missed as they ducked behind cover.

I tsked, getting to my bike, turning it on as I realized that Bren wasn't sitting on it. His eyes kept going up and down like he couldn't believe what was happening.

Meanwhile, I couldn't believe that he was hesitating right at the moment when I needed him to come with me.

"Look, I don't like having to save you any more than you do, but those guys killed your bodyguards and our fathers. We don't have another choice. We need to go to your house and, when we get there, you won't have to ever see me again, I promise."

I was actually looking forward to that.

He nodded, swinging his leg over the motorcycle as he wrapped his arms around my torso. I felt warmth in my heart as he did that, almost like I was enjoying it. But I shouldn't be feeling that way about it, I thought.

I twisted the handlebars of the motorcycle, stepped on it,

and then rode away as fast as I could to where his house was. He lived in a mansion far from where we were. It was going to take me a lot of time to get there.

I heard bullets whizzing past our ears as I kept on speeding up Desire. I pulled out my pistol, turned around without taking my hand off the left handlebar of the motorcycle, and then popped some shots in the heads of the bikers that were chasing us.

Bren ducked and buried his head on my back, tightening his arms around me. I wasn't going to deny that I felt a little sorry for him and better about him than I ever did in my life.

I studied the roads behind us as I realized that the bikers weren't chasing us anymore. I eased my grip on the handlebars of the motorcycle, turned to the left, and then cruised toward his house.

I had no idea how his Omega father was going to take it, but I was sure he was going to be better there.

CHAPTER 3

Bren

The fact that he was taking me to my house instead of abandoning me was a lot more than I expected from him. I was still with my arms wrapped around his torso and I wasn't thinking about pulling myself away from him anytime soon. The fact was that I needed someone to make me feel safe, even if it was the person I most hated in my life.

My father just died and he died thinking I hated him. I hated myself because I didn't tell him how important he was to me.

I should have told him that I was okay with his traditions and that we could work something out. Maybe I could have convinced him about marrying me to Ish instead.

But it was too late now for that, I thought as a tear rolled down my cheek. I pulled my head back as I studied the environment around me.

We were already leaving downtown and I couldn't even see cars or other bikes near us. It was almost like we were alone here or that someone was watching us.

"You can take your arms off my body now," Cogwyn growled, his earring blinking under the moonlight. It wasn't a full moon and I knew that he wasn't going to turn, thank goodness. I wouldn't know what to do if he did.

"But I'll fall off the bike if I do that."

He twisted the handlebars of the motorcycle as he sped through a red light. I widened my eyes, looking flabbergasted that he did that.

"No, you won't, and I don't like it when people like you get attached to me."

"You just rode through a red light. That's an infraction."

Cogwyn blinked twice, almost like he couldn't believe that I just said that. Then, he started to laugh as he turned his attention back to the road.

"Of course I did that. Did you think I was going to follow all the rules of how to drive properly when we're running for our lives?"

He peeked over his shoulder, his smirk taunting me and making me hate him more than I already did. Seeing that, I pushed myself away from him and gripped the sides of his motorcycle.

Fine. If he was going to keep being the asshole he'd always been, then I wanted as much distance from him as possible, even if that meant possibly hurting myself.

I was gripping the sides of his motorcycle as tightly as I could, so I was hoping it wasn't going to come to that. He did slow down his motorcycle, still cruising in the streets. I saw buildings and the houses moving past us, the golden and glowing light bulbs making the city look less gritty in the dark.

My heart was still in pain. My mind kept going back to my father.

After a moment, the biker turned his head to look at me through the corner of his right eye. "Look, I'm sorry about what happened. After we call the police and they sort this out, we'll go back there and bury our fathers. Everything will be better then."

"I don't believe you," I said through gritted teeth. The last thing I wanted right now was to start bonding with him, even if he was hot and my type. I never told anyone about this, but I liked bad boys more than I liked admitting that to myself.

Not to mention that his body was very warm when I was hugging him from behind.

"Believe me or don't, I know that everything will be better. You think I'm not in pain that they killed my father?" He said. "I'm going to get my revenge, one way or the other. I'll find out who did that and who ordered the attack, and then I'll kill every last one of them."

I believed him when he said that. I believed that he was going to seek revenge when he was feeling better.

He sped through another red light as I started to feel a strong scent in the air. Then, seconds later, I started to hear the rumbling of the motorcycle's engine. I snapped my head to look behind my shoulder as I realized that it was one of the Bear Bikers that was coming for us.

He twisted the handlebars of his motorcycle and it accelerated toward us. I was going to warn Cogwyn when he snapped his head to return his attention to the road in front of us.

"I saw him. Don't worry. I'm going to lose him."

Without thinking about it twice, I threw my arms around his body and hugged him tightly. He didn't say anything as he sped up the motorcycle and took us as far away from the pursuing biker as he could.

His motorcycle was trembling underneath us and, alongside Cogwyn, it was the only thing making me feel as safe as I could feel.

He swerved to the right and then to the left, entering another street. "How long until we get home?" I asked, raising my voice so that it could be heard through the rumbling of the motorcycle. I still didn't know what its name was, but I was pretty sure that he had named it. Every biker did that.

"Not much longer-" he was saying when a shot came from behind us, his body twitching for a second. I snapped my head up, wondering what just happened. Then, I started to feel something warm and liquid pooling on my chest.

Moments later, pain was flooding my body and I started to lose strength. My vision was darkening and I had no idea what was happening. All I knew was that Cogwyn was still riding us on his motorcycle and accelerating it as much as he could while also trying to lose our pursuer.

He swerved the motorcycle to the left, snapping his head to look over his shoulder. "I heard a shot. Are you feeling okay? Your arms are moving away from me. You need to hold on tight–"

Just as he was saying that, I couldn't keep doing what I was doing any longer. I couldn't keep hugging him. My body was losing strength and my vision was still getting darker.

Cogwyn started to slow down the motorcycle as he realized what was happening. I saw his eyes going wide as he noticed that I was falling off the motorcycle. It was still going pretty fast across the road and I knew that if I fell off of it, I'd die or get badly hurt.

"Bren!" He yelled, his hand snatching mine and yanking me back to the motorcycle. I could feel the rising pain in my chest, just underneath my heart. They could have killed me then. I didn't know why the Bear Bikers were still chasing us, but they were.

The rumbling of motorcycles' engines grew louder, now coming from all directions behind us. I looked over my shoulder and realized that more bikers were coming for us this time.

They looked determined, hungry, and were even transforming. They were between being humans and bears now. They couldn't keep riding their motorcycles if they finished their transformations. They would only transform if they needed to fight hand-to-hand.

"I'm not letting you fall off the bike," Cogwyn yelled, speeding up his motorcycle as the wind blew my hair behind my head. I was happy that he was gripping my hand so tightly and could still keep riding his motorcycle as if nothing bad was happening.

When it came down to it, it was obvious that he'd been in

this kind of situation before. He was used to it.

"I'm going to take a shortcut. There's a place where we can hide and I can patch you up," he said, taking the left, entering an alleyway, and then another and one more. Before long, I couldn't hear or smell the bikers that had been chasing us.

I was pretty sure that they were still searching for us, but right now we should be okay. The motorcycle was gliding across the alleyway, stopping when we reached a building. It looked rundown, and it had broken windows and the paint was cracking and flaking off the walls.

Cogwyn turned off the engine of the motorcycle, wrapping one arm around me and pulling me off of it. "You might not like me and that's fine, but right now, I'm the only one who can help you."

He took me off the bike, his hand going for his pocket as he palmed it. "Shit, looks like I even forgot my phone in the church. I suppose they also didn't let you in with yours, right?" He asked, making me remember that a couple of workers did take care of the place.

They were probably dead now.

I shook my head, my vision going completely dark this time as I lost my consciousness. The only hope I had of pulling through this was this wolf shifter actually being more than who he appeared to be.

And I hoped that his intentions were really good.

CHAPTER 4

Cogwyn

He took a shot to his stomach and was bleeding pretty badly. I dragged him up to the second floor of the building, opened the door, laid him down on the bed, and then looked out the window to make sure that nobody was coming here.

The alleyway where the building was located was silent and peaceful, a page of a newspaper flying in the wind.

I closed the window, turned on the fan, and then started to patch up his wound. Bren didn't know this, but I used to go to medical school before dropping out of it and becoming a biker. A lot of things happened since then and I didn't want to remember them. I was just happy that I knew how to treat a wound as serious as his.

He was bleeding so bad I was worried he wasn't going to pull through. I had a first-aid kit tucked in one of the dressers. I only came to this building when I had a lot on my mind and needed to think about things.

I opened the first-aid kit, grabbed everything that was in it, and then started to dress his wound after taking out the bullet.

He groaned, turning around in the bed as I noticed that I was going to have to change the bedsheets. Blood was soaking them red. I checked his pulse and was happy that it was still strong.

Even though Bren bled a lot, I was confident he had a good chance of pulling through.

Still, I was worried now and still thinking about my father. I fisted my hand as I promised myself again I was going to get my revenge, no matter what happened.

I pushed that thought out and focused on the matter at hand. I looped the gauze dressings around his torso, turned him around, and then checked his pulse again to make sure it was still strong.

After determining that it was, I pulled a chair over and plopped down on it, and started to look at Bren with no particular intention in mind. I was just gazing at him, time passing, and I was happy that he was feeling better. I wouldn't say that he was already okay, but there was no denying that the ointments I applied on his wound and the gauze dressings were already working their magic.

I jumped off the chair when I heard a motorcycle's engine speeding up far from here. It was probably one of the Bear Bikers who was hunting in the area for us. I was feeling pretty safe where I was.

It was unlikely they would find this place. This part of the city was always dark, filled with alleyways after alleyways, narrow roads, and other gangs that controlled it.

Dammit. If only I had my phone with me – or his phone – I'd be calling my mates to help me with this. They'd come running over here as fast as they could and they'd put those bikers back in their place. They needed to be killed – all of them.

I groaned, checking Bren out. No denying that he was cute and a sight for sore eyes, especially when he was sleeping. The biggest problem with him was that he was always a snobby asshole.

He always thought that he was better than most people just because he was more educated, more intelligent, and more 'cultured,' or whatever that was supposed to mean.

My body was relaxed on the chair, sunk in it. My clothes were soaked in sweat. Time passed and all I was doing was to keep looking at the Omega on the bed.

It felt good to be gazing at him like this when I knew he didn't know I was doing that. After all, I didn't want him to find out I thought he was cute.

I closed my eyes and when I reopened them, he was already sitting up on the bed. Supporting himself with his arms, he glanced at me, his eyes going wide.

Then, his hand started to palm the gauze dressings on his torso.

"You got shot in the stomach, but I think you're going to be okay. I don't have my phone with me and I'm not going out and risk getting caught. We need to stay here for the time being."

For a moment, Bren didn't say anything. He was staring at me and the way he was doing that was making me feel uncomfortable. It was like he never thought I'd help him as much as I did.

"You dressed my wound and saved me."

I nodded, smiling softly. "I did those things." After a moment of silence, I said, "and I'm expecting at least a thank you."

He pursed his lips, looking away from me. Well, Bren was never going to stop being the person I knew he was. Always snobby, always looking down on people like me, and always thinking that I was nothing more than a criminal.

I wasn't going to deny I did some things considered illegal, but I was also much more than that.

And here our parents were thinking we were fated mates and that we were going to get married like they did. We were so different. He preferred spending most of his time studying, locked up in his room, and pretending that the rest of the world didn't exist. Meanwhile, I was all about the thrills and making the most out of my life.

"Being grumpy like that isn't going to help us. We need to

wait it out."

He pushed himself off the bed, standing up and losing his balance right after that.

"I'm not going to stay here another second with you," he grumbled as he fell into my arms after I leaped from the chair where I was sitting.

Bren could be as grumpy as he wanted to be, but it wasn't going to change who I was. I was going to help him and then I was going to drop him off at his house, and that was going to be the end of it. After that, I needed to bury my father and then avenge his death. Just thinking about it, I felt my heart tight.

"Whoa there, Bren. You're not ready to go out yet. You can't even get off the bed. Your body is in pain and you know it."

He looked away, pushing himself off of me. He lied on the bed and started to stare at the ceiling.

"This is like my worst dream becoming real. I'm in the same room with you, I can't leave the building, and you helped me even though you didn't need to. It's like you're trying to tell me you are much more than the biker who hurts other people."

A moment later, I decided to ignore that.

I shook my head, stepping away from him. I opened the door to the bathroom, turned on the faucet, and I was happy when water started to come out from the showerhead. At least we had running water in the building.

"You can thank me later when you're feeling better. You know, I think I prefer it when you are sleeping more and talking less."

Bren grunted, crossing his arms over his chest and then turning around so that his back was facing me. I shook my head, took off my clothes, closed the door of the bathroom, and then stepped under the showerhead.

The water running around my body was already making me feel a lot better. I started to soap myself up and then I applied shampoo to my hair, not thinking about anything that didn't involve avenging my father.

I rinsed my body with the water and then stepped out from under the showerhead. I dried my body with the towel and then threw my clothes back on.

I opened the door to the bedroom again and I wasn't surprised when I found out that Bren was still with his back turned to me.

And here I was hoping he was going to change and become someone better. It looked like he was helpless when it came to that. He was always going to be grumpy and snobby.

And then, I heard a slight snoring coming from him. He was sleeping, which relieved me. It meant that he wasn't going to try to flee from the building when we weren't ready yet. We still needed to wait until the Bear Bikers got tired of hunting for us.

Bren was sleeping in the only bed we had. That meant I only had the chair to take a nap on, and knowing that didn't bother me. I had slept in worse places.

CHAPTER 5

Bren

I cracked my eyes open as I realized I was still in the same room, my heart tight even though I had no idea why. I sat up on the bed as I looked around and noticed that light streaks were coming through the window. It was the only window in this old, dusty room.

The smell in it was horrible, making me feel terrible. Not even the Alpha's scent was strong enough to make being in this place more bearable.

He was seated on the chair by my side, almost like he was trying to prove to me he cared about my wellbeing. It didn't matter that he dressed my wound. He wasn't going to fool me. Cogwyn was still the same asshole who used to bully me when I was in school. He was a couple of years older than me.

But that was just one of the many reasons why I didn't like him.

It was morning and I was already feeling much better, even though I didn't want to admit that it was thanks to him. I pushed myself off the bed and then started to walk on my tiptoes to the door. I wrapped my hand on the doorknob, pushed it open, and then looked over my shoulder.

Was I really going to do this? I asked myself, realizing that I was abandoning the only person who was helping me since the attack.

Sure, he would never stop being the asshole he was, a criminal who did the most unspeakable things, but he was still my only chance at getting home safely.

What was I going to do in this neighborhood, where everyone was Betas and they didn't like Omegas like us? I didn't know how to ride his motorcycle, even though I could try to learn on the fly. Not to mention that his motorcycle's key was probably in his pocket…

If I went over to him slowly and carefully, there would still be a good chance he would hear me. I was light, but not like a feather.

I groaned softly, closing the door when his eyelids opened slowly. Oh, fuck. Cogwyn was already waking up. He was going to see that I was trying to flee and mock me for not going through with it. It was going to be just like in school. He was going to say that I didn't have the courage to do it.

I sped over back to the bed on my tip-toes, hiding the fact that part of me felt thankful that he helped me. And also hiding one more thing which couldn't come to light, no matter what happened – Cogwyn was such a hottie! Even back in school, I thought that way about him.

He was my type. When I fell into his arms that time, I melted in them and, for a moment, I couldn't think about anything that didn't involve him holding me like that, telling me that everything was going to be okay. That was something that only bad boys like him could do.

Cogwyn pushed himself up off the chair, noticing me. I straightened up my spine as I smiled from ear to ear, trying to make it look like I wasn't doing what I was.

"You weren't trying to escape, or were you?" He probed, marching toward me. He was much bigger and taller than me. His fur was growing back, his eyes turning yellow as the shape of his pupils changed. He checked me out from bottom to top, disdain in his eyes. "And here I've been doing everything in my power to make you feel better. I should just kick you out to the Bears."

I whimpered, scurrying away from him as fast as I could. His muscles appeared to be growing bigger, harder, and his tattoos seemed to be getting stretched.

When I felt my butt touching the wall, I knew I didn't have any more room to wriggle around and escape from Cogwyn. He had me cornered.

And yet, I knew that he wasn't going to hurt me.

His fur went back into his body and his pupils returned to their normal shape. Sitting on the bed, he looked at me and made a movement with his hand, asking me to sit there with him.

"You don't have to like me and I'm not asking that you do, but we still need to help each other. Here. Come here. There's a lot we need to talk about."

Maybe it was his strong and intense Alpha scent that was doing it, but I started to step over to him slowly. I almost felt like the distance between us was growing larger.

Eventually, I sat on the bed as he repeated, "I know we don't like each other, but we need to work together."

And the way he said that made me feel that he was being genuine about it. Still, it was difficult for me to take him seriously, even though I knew the gravity of our situation well.

I couldn't help but feel something for him which I was assuming was connected to the fact I was an Omega. His scent was strong and very intense, drawing me to him. He took a shower last night and was smelling very nice this morning. He didn't even spray on perfume, but his smell was still exactly what I thought it was going to be after a hot shower.

"I'm trying to do that..." I mumbled, leaning toward him even though I knew I shouldn't be doing that. After all, what was he planning on doing now? Was he going to hurt me? And why was I even thinking that after he dressed my wound?

Truth was that he was hot, was being very caring with me right now, and was pretty much pushing every button that turned me on. It was like time was moving in slow motion for me as my head neared his head, his eyes locking with my eyes, my lips parting, and then... I realized the weight of what was happening.

At that moment, I jumped off the bed and strode away from him. I crossed my arms around my chest as I mumbled, "We're going to help each other out as much as we can, but no more than that."

A moment passed and Cogwyn didn't say anything, letting silence fill the void between us. He knew what happened and he wasn't stupid. He knew that we were almost kissing. He straightened up his spine, showing me that he was also leaning into me for a kiss.

That realization made me widen my eyes right away. Did that mean he also found me hot? That couldn't be. Cogwyn had been with several Omegas in his life and I was just one of many.

Not to mention that I couldn't be his type. He always said that I thought I was better than everyone else and was a snobby asshole.

After a while, he said, "Should we go out now? I think we should be in the clear."

I looked around and remembered that I was going to have to hug him from behind again, and that thought made me not want to go out with him right now.

I bit my lower lip, saying, "I think I want to wait a little while longer."

"And you want to stay in this dump for a couple more minutes with me?" He asked, crossing his arms over his chest as he looked down on me. "I thought you were beyond that. I mean, you've always said that the last thing you wanted to do is to live in a place like this for more than a day."

I whirled around, meeting his eyes. I thought I was going to see the eyes of someone who hated me, but I was seeing the opposite. I supposed that was because we were going through the same thing.

Both of our fathers died yesterday and we were still trying to cope with that. Not to mention that we were finally sharing another room that wasn't a classroom.

"This isn't about that. I've changed. I'm not the same person."

"Of course you aren't. You can't wait until the moment you don't have to spend another second with me."

"You know what?" I barked, raising my voice. "I'm not staying here another minute. I'm not staying here because you're being an asshole even though you don't have to be. I didn't give you any reasons to be like that to me." I threw the door open and stormed out of the room, eventually reaching the stairs and then the door out of the building.

Moments later, I felt a hand snatching me up and putting me on a motorcycle.

CHAPTER 6

Cogwyn

When I realized what was happening, it was already too late. One of the Bear Bikers, Dyson, popped out of nowhere and snatched Bren before I even knew what was happening. One moment he was outside the building and the next he was riding away on a motorcycle.

I stormed out of the building and stood where I was, frozen in place. I was helping Bren because I felt sorry for him, but then I realized it meant something more. I felt something more for him, like we really were fated mates.

I shook my head, rushed over to Desire, sat on it, and then rode off after them. My heart was in my throat. I shouldn't even be doing this.

It wasn't that I only thought of myself most of the time, but that I felt something for Bren that made me jealous for him.

As usual, I didn't put on my helmet as I didn't think it was necessary and I didn't like it. This time, though, I was doing it also because I needed to catch up to the other biker as soon as possible.

If I didn't do that, I had no idea what would happen to Bren. He needed my help and I was willing to risk my life to provide it.

Moments later, when I was speeding up my motorcycle, I finally spotted them in the distance. They were far from me, but not impossible to reach. I twisted the handlebars of the motorcycle, accelerating it to its limits. The engine was rumbling and the motorcycle itself was trembling, but I knew it was going to be okay.

When I was about to reach them, Dyson turned his head and pulled out his shotgun. It was a sawed-off shotgun, and he pulled the trigger with the gun right above Bren's head.

I thought about what was going to happen and how loud the shotgun was going to be, and my heart was tighter all of a sudden because I couldn't do anything to stop him.

But there was at least one thing I could try to do to help the Omega. "Bren!" I shouted, being loud enough to be heard through the engines of the motorcycles. "Cover your ears and duck. He's going to shoot."

"What?" He squeaked and even though I wasn't able to hear what he said, I knew that's what came out of his mouth. He was holding on tightly to Dyson but as soon as he realized he was pulling up his shotgun, he obeyed me, ducking and covering his ears with his hands.

I swerved to the right as I had just about enough time to judge where the bullets were going to hit. Most of all, right now I was worried for his safety. Bren was feeling better, but he still needed to rest.

I cursed Dyson for showing up. He always thought he was my nemesis. I always looked down on him because he was always nothing more than a nuisance. This time, he was pissing me off. It was like he was stealing Bren from me.

I was more surprised than anything I was feeling this way about it. After all, the old me would have already given up on him and let him be captured by the Bear Bikers.

The bullets hit the pavement and I had just about enough time to escape them, and also enough time to pull out my pistol and point it to Dyson's head. I didn't feel anything as I approached them on my motorcycle and pulled the trigger.

Dyson didn't have enough time to react. His hands let go of the motorcycle's handlebars, the motorcycle itself swerving left and right crazily. I threw my arm around Bren's body and pulled him to me. Dyson's motorcycle lost its balance, flipped across the pavement, and I put the Omega on the backseat.

After riding for a couple of minutes as he wrapped his arms around my chest and buried his head on my back, I finally pulled over when I felt that nobody was chasing us anymore.

Dyson had always been like that. He preferred to work on his own whenever he could. This time, I felt that he was doing that because the leader of the Bear Bikers told them to spread out throughout the neighborhood.

When I pulled over and turned off the engine of the motorcycle, I eased up my body and let out a sigh. I peeked behind my shoulder, loving the fact that Bren was still holding on so tightly to me. It was like he was telling me, even though he didn't mean to, that I was the only person who could make him feel safe right now.

That moment when we almost kissed... It was still in my mind even though he did what he did moments later. He said those awful things to my face, treating me like I was less than trash.

The old me would be dumping his ass right now and forgetting about his existence, especially now that the Sphere of Revelations didn't exist anymore. We weren't even able to hear what it was going to say, if we were fated mates or not.

When the Omega couldn't hear the rumbling of the motorcycles' engines anymore, he looked up and pushed himself away from me. I just realized that my fur was growing and that my teeth were getting bigger.

There were so many times when I couldn't control my transformation. I didn't want to let it happen because I always lost control of myself when it happened.

"What even happened?" He asked, and he was feeling so

much fear I could hear his heart pounding in his chest.

"I just saved you again. That's what happened," I said, tucking my pistol back in the holster.

He blinked twice, pushing himself away from me further and getting off the bike. As he walked away from me, I asked him, "Are you going back to your house on your own? Do you really want to put a big target on your Omega father's head? Do you want to live with that?"

Bren stopped in his tracks, turning his head to look at me.

"If you are baiting me to stay another day with you, forget it. It's not going to happen."

"You say that like I'm not aware of it." I sighed, getting off my bike and marching toward him. When I stopped in front of him, I realized yet again I was much taller than him. "The truth is that you shouldn't go back to your house. I just realized that doing so would be a mistake. We don't even have news about what happened – if anything happened – in his house. By now, he probably already knows that his husband is dead."

Bren parted his lips and I thought he was going to say something when, suddenly, he threw his arms around me and hugged me tightly, burying his head in my chest.

"I just hate all this. I hate the fated mates thing. I hate the bear bikers, I hate the wolf shifters, and I hate you."

I was taken by surprise by what he did, but eventually I was used to it. I wrapped my arms around his body and hugged him as well. I didn't say anything, just letting Bren whimper and cry against my chest. If it was making him feel better and helping him cope with what happened, then I was feeling better, too.

It was the first time I was feeling so connected to him. We lived such different lives I thought this moment would never happen. It took our fathers dying on the same night to make me better understand what was going on in his mind.

When he pulled back, but without taking his arms off of me, he locked his eyes with me and I knew that this was the moment where he was thinking the same thing I was.

I moved my right hand over his spine, entangling my fingers in his hair. I pulled his head up and we connected our lips, washing away all the bad memories we were collecting since our fathers died. His lips were very sweet, just like I always thought they were. The truth was, I had always had a little crush on him.

And now I was fulfilling that crush by kissing him. He melted in my arms, moaning into my mouth. I slid my tongue between his lips and then pulled him more tightly against me, needing to feel his body and how warm it was.

Our tongues battled for control for a couple of minutes until I won the battle, letting a moment of nothingness pass so that he could catch his breath.

And when he locked his eyes with me again, I knew that things were taking a turn for the better between us.

CHAPTER 7

Bren

I never thought I'd kiss him and much less take him to my home. Even though he was right when he said that the Bear Bikers would have come here for my other father, they didn't.

I opened the door of my room for Cogwyn, opening my mouth when I was going to offer him some food. But he just lifted his hand, going to the bathroom.

"I'm going to take a shower first."

I didn't need to invite him to do that because he was always pushy like that. He opened the door of the bathroom and then closed it behind him, almost like this was his bedroom.

Even though I never thought he would ever take a shower in my own house, I was happy that he was. When I thought about it, I just couldn't deny the growing feeling in my heart that I was beginning to like him – and I was making sure I was stressing out that it didn't involve anything more than that.

After all, we kissed and it was just a moment where we needed to wash away all the bad things that were in our minds. Seated on the bed, I kept moving my hand over the bedsheets as I remembered everything that happened between me and my father. My last words to him must have hurt him more than I thought they did at the time.

In the meantime, I had no idea what I was going to do next. I thought that I did the right thing by inviting Cogwyn to live with me for a little while, even though I knew it was unlikely he was going to accept it.

The sun was already setting behind the buildings and I knew that he was only going to sleep with me tonight because he didn't have another place to go to. I mean, he had that rundown building in that neighborhood, but I didn't think he was very fond of it.

Minutes later, when my eyes were closed, he opened the door of the bathroom and I noticed that he was shirtless, his towel wrapped around the lower part of his body.

I couldn't help but check him out from bottom to top, realizing that my Omega side was now speaking louder than my common sense. I shouldn't and couldn't get involved with him. I knew it would only bring pain.

Cogwyn was rubbing his hair with a towel as he went over to the dresser, where I had said I had left some clothes for him. I had no idea if he was going to choose to wear them, but they were better than the worn clothes he had with him. They were smelly and even though I didn't like them at all, I couldn't help but admit that I wanted to take a sniff of them one day, if I ever found myself alone to do that.

After he finished rubbing his hair with the towel, he turned and walked over to me. I scooted away from him on the bed, and he noticed that. He stopped before sitting down on the mattress, and I noticed the bed sagging as he put all his weight on it.

I was still moving away from him when he grabbed my hand, making me snap my head to look at his eyes. They were determined and intense eyes that were staring at me as if he was reading my mind.

"Do you want to talk about it?" He asked, the way he was gripping my hand feeling determined. I felt that, if I wanted to move my hand away from him, he wouldn't hesitate before showing me that he didn't accept that. Everything that I wondered about us was beginning to show me that it was true.

This big wolf shifter had the same feelings for me I had for him, and it was difficult for me to process that in my mind. Moments later, he finally eased his grip on my hand and I exhaled.

I supposed there was no point in pretending I didn't kiss him. I did and it was going to be something that was going to forever be in my mind.

"I don't think we should," I responded, looking at his eyes, but I held my gaze only for a fraction of a second. As an Alpha, he was dominating even when all we were doing was looking at each other and talking. As an Omega, I was always going to be submissive. Sometimes I was also rebellious, but most of the time, I was submissive.

"Why not? I know that a lot happened in our lives because of the attack – and believe me when I say I'm going to avenge our fathers – but you just showed me something I thought would never happen. You always showed me how much you hated me for being different, for not following in my father's footsteps."

Cogwyn was right. His father was one of the most influential CEOs in the country and one of the reasons why he was able to choose this lifestyle over following in his father's footsteps.

Without his money and the influence he had, he would probably have died in the biker gang's initiation process. I heard it was pretty rough.

I could smell his scent and that it was growing more intense as time passed. Likewise, my cock was growing bigger under my pants. I still had to take a shower myself and I knew I was a little smelly, but Cogwyn wasn't letting that stop him. I knew that he was naked and that the only thing preventing me from peeking at his cock was his towel.

I took a deep breath in, his arm wrapping around me as he pulled me in for a kiss. We were picking up from where we left off, I thought, melting in his embrace. My hand went for his thigh, and I slid it under the towel, feeling the smoothness of his skin.

I thought that kissing someone so despicable, a biker that could become a wolf at will, would make me feel like puking, but it was the opposite that was happening.

Perhaps it was the tragic events that happened that were making this feel so much better. It was the only thing that made me feel like it all happened years ago, that I was already over it even though I didn't even bury my father yet.

He slid his tongue into my mouth, pushing me down against the bed. He climbed on top of me, his hand pulling my shirt up as I grabbed his arms. Our eyes locked as he asked, "You don't want to do this anymore?"

I bit my bottom lip, finally answering, "It's not that. It's just that..."

He widened his eyes slightly. He was realizing something about me I had always kept under wraps. I just didn't want anyone to find out about it until the time was right.

"Don't tell me that you are..." He mumbled, making my heart speed up. I thought that he was going to jump away from me and walk out of my house, but he was still there when I reopened my eyes after closing them.

And then, his lips were connecting to mine again.

"That's so silly. I love it that you are that way," he purred, his muscles bulging as he started to feel my body with his hands. He had just finished taking off my shirt and I felt exposed that I was naked before him, time passing slowly. I loved that time was cooperating with us right now.

As he moved, the towel slid off of his body and finally revealed to me what I had been thinking about this whole time. It was all happening so suddenly and I was falling in love with him so quickly it was unbelievable that things were happening this way.

My eyes darted down to his cock and I drew in a short breath when I saw just how big it was. Not just big, but also thick and mean. It was hot, hard, and pointing right at me.

He was cut like I was, a smile flashing on his face as he realized that what was happening was already beyond our control.

He moved his hand up, pinched my nipple, and then started to work to take off my belt. Moments later, when I was already past trying to stop this, he took off my belt and started to lower my pants.

I pushed him away from me – or at least, I tried to – as I realized I hadn't done something very important, but it appeared that he was reading my mind just like I thought he was going to.

He lowered his head, murmuring into my ear, "Don't worry, Bren. I closed the door."

CHAPTER 8

Cogwyn

My heart was pounding in my head as I realized the weight of what was happening. I was kissing this Omega, finally doing something with him I thought would never happen. I just finished taking off his pants and now it was time to take off his underwear, too. He had a pair of dark boxer briefs on, and underneath it I could see the shadow that his cock made. It was a little on the small side, but I thought it was perfect for me.

I kissed Bren again, groping his chest and feeling his perfect little abs. I moved my hands down, ripped off his boxer briefs, and then grabbed his cock. Just one hand was enough.

My teeth were growing pointier and I knew that the other side of me wanted to come out. I pushed him back, keeping him away from this. I was going to knot this rebellious Omega and he was going to be mine, no matter what happened.

I was in his house and everything should be fine here. I thought that the Bear Bikers had already mounted an attack against this place but, thankfully, that didn't happen.

I kicked those thoughts out of my mind as they didn't have any place in here right now. I could hear his raggedy, uncontrolled breathing. Bren was finally, for a couple of minutes, not the uptight asswipe he'd always been. Hell, he even looked like a completely changed person himself.

I had this uncontrollable urge to knot him and it wasn't even popping up in my mind that I should probably wear a condom. I was just devouring his neck with impossible, long kisses, feeling the warmth of his body and how it was everything I wanted right now.

I was going to knot this Omega and nothing was going to stop me.

I stroked his dick for what felt like hours, his body squirming and convulsing when he orgasmed. His milk came out in long, hot ropes all over his body, some of them even hitting my belly. I lowered my head and lapped them up. I scooped up his jelly on my belly with my finger and then brought it to my mouth, licking it.

"It's wonderful, and you're delicious," I groaned, moving over his body and going down on his dick. I enclosed my lips around his little cockhead, giving the underside of it long and controlled licks that brought him over the edge again. Bren grabbed my hair however he could, grinding his body against mine as he convulsed again and again. I almost thought he was going to pass out, but it didn't happen.

He was still right here with me and I was holding his head, sweat pooling on his forehead.

"Do that again, please," he murmured, his lips brushing over mine when he attempted to kiss me again. I could only do what he was requesting of me, his hand going for my dick and grabbing it. He gave it a couple of strokes, his eyes wide when he realized how big I was.

I pecked his neck one more time and he threw his legs around my body, pinning me down against him. I groaned into his mouth, rubbing my balls against his nuts as I felt that familiar sensation that preceded an orgasm. But I wasn't going to climax until the right moment.

My nails were growing bigger, the transformation happening despite my efforts. I could only knot him when I was inside of him, so I didn't worry that anything I didn't like was going to happen.

I moved down over his body again, playing with his balls as he threw his head backward, coming for the third time in a row. This time, his hot and creamy sperm hit all over my face, and I scooped up everything I could with my fingers. I licked them off one by one, my eyes locked with my Omega's.

That turned him on, his cheeks redder. I gave his ballsack a little tug and then turned him around. He was already wet and clenching for me, just waiting for me to penetrate him. As the good-natured Alpha I was – I chuckled at that thought – I lapped up his juices and then grabbed his thighs.

I pulled him to me slowly, lining up my dick to his tunnel before nudging it. Moments later, I thrust in with greater force and then penetrated him. I slid in all the way, bottoming him out.

When I was all the way inside of him, seeing only my balls right now, I lowered my head and murmured into his ear, "Does it hurt too much?"

He shook his head, giving me the okay to go on. I started to roll my hips, my hands holding his body over the bed. I was letting time pass so that he was used to my size. Meanwhile, he was clenching me tightly and I knew that I'd only pull out of him after coming and impregnating him.

The thing about us being fated mates was just a mere memory in my mind right now, and I didn't give it much thought. I focused on pounding in and out of him slowly, picking up speed when I realized that he was much better used to my size.

My dick grew bigger, my balls slapping off of his asscheeks when I could feel my sperm coming out. When it exploded and orgasm swept through my body, I dug my fingers deeper into his thighs and pulled him more tightly against mine.

I knotted the Omega.

My dick throbbed and erupted inside of his tunnel, the

thought that I was getting him pregnant feeling so right – even though we didn't plan for this and it would be unlikely he wouldn't hate me after this.

Minutes later, my orgasm faded when my shaft returned to its normal size. My body was sated and now it felt that I could finally pull out of him. And so I did that, plopping down on the bed as he did the same thing.

Bren had his back turned to me and, for a moment, while my dick was still getting softer, I thought something bad had happened. Maybe he was finally realizing that he didn't want to get pregnant and that I was an asshole for doing that.

I put my arm around him and pulled him to me, his eyes looking at me as I realized that tears were coming out of them. I slid my hand over his cheek, asking, "Something happened? You look distressed."

"I think... my father might have been right about it. We were made for each other, weren't we? We are fated mates. That's what the sphere was going to tell us."

I was caressing his cheek when I said, "Hey, no need to cry right now. I know what happened and what it means to you. I don't know what the sphere would have said, but I think it's irrelevant right now anyway. You just showed me a side of you I thought you didn't have. You showed me that you aren't just the snobby asshole I always thought you were."

Bren chuckled. "Thanks... I think I want to say that I'm beginning to like you."

He was still having difficulty breathing, his chest expanding and contracting slowly and noticeably. I pulled him more tightly against me, my dick already hard as I thought about fucking him again.

I knew that it wasn't going to happen – at least, not right now – but the thought was still in my mind, and my mind could always be changed.

"That's much better than who you were like before. I felt like you could have slit my throat while I was sleeping."

"For a good reason. You were always putting me down when we were younger."

"Well, now we're grownups and we know better than doing that, don't you agree?" I brushed my lips against his lips again, biting his upper lip for a fraction of a second. He moaned, pushing his body closer against mine. I was so surprised by the way he was taking this I thought he never would.

"So, how was it like, losing your virginity with me?" I quizzed, just holding him against me and really feeling like we were fated mates, just like that dumb sphere was going to tell us.

"It was amazing," he crooned, snuggling up on me as we cuddled and fell asleep. I never said this to Bren, but it was the best sleep I had in a while. I couldn't help but feel impatient about what the future held in store for us, despite all the other bad things that came with that attack.

I still needed to find out everything about it, even though I was already looking forward to a life together with Bren.

CHAPTER 9

Bren

I was in his arms when I woke up, turning to the right in the bed as I noticed the photo of my parents on the nightstand. One of my fathers – the one that survived and was still living in our house – didn't approve of Cogwyn at all.

I always felt connected to him and that I could understand him, but now that I was in Cogwyn's strong arms, I couldn't look at him the same way. I couldn't help but think he was the Alpha I didn't even know I was looking for.

I sighed, not wishing to turn this into an argument I couldn't win. Ranulf was a good man, but even the night before he already told me that he didn't want Cogwyn to spend another night in our place.

I told him that I understood why he said that, but now that it was the next morning and the sunlight was shining brightly through the windows, I couldn't help but wonder if maybe he couldn't be convinced otherwise.

I fisted my hand, thinking about my dead Alpha father. If Ranulf was there, he'd be dead right now too, and I would never have forgiven myself. I should be happy that he was here and alive. At least we could mourn together.

We still needed to go over the procedures involving the burial of our fathers, and I could already tell that it wasn't going to be pretty. One of the reasons for that was that Ranulf wasn't going to think twice before spouting that he didn't want Cogwyn's father to be buried near his husband.

Either way, I never thought that was going to happen anyway. Cogwyn was going to choose a different cemetery for his father's final resting place.

I was going to make sure that I was going to be there for him regardless, though. He deserved that much from me.

I picked up the portrait with all three of us in it, brushed my finger over the photo, and then shimmed out of Cogwyn's heavy arms. He groaned, turning so that his back was facing me.

I still couldn't believe that I lost my virginity to my bully. He was so incredible. I thought that it was going to happen with my boyfriend, but he'd always been postponing it. I didn't know why, but he never looked forward to us having sex.

I got off the bed and then went to the shower, still stealing glances at the huge man in my bed. Did he knock me up and did that mean I was going to have his baby – or many? I didn't know, but I was still under the effects of the fact that I lost my virginity and I couldn't be any happier. I'd only be happier if that attack hadn't happened.

Perhaps my father had always been right about one thing – some things always happened for a reason. I didn't want to think about it this way, but maybe the attack happened so that Cogwyn and I could learn we were different than who we thought...

I went to the shower room, opened the door, and then started to take a shower. As the water flowed around my body and then down to the drain, I was already feeling even better. I had sex with Cogwyn when I was smelly and dirty. I couldn't help but look forward to when we could do it when I was smelling better.

I chuckled at that thought as I walked out of the shower room, rubbing a towel on my hair until it was dry. I just finished putting on my clothes when I heard a groan coming from the bed. I snapped my head to it as I realized that Cogwyn was waking up.

Even though I still had to explain to Ish that things between us were going to be different from now on, I was really looking forward to having many mornings like this one in the future.

It would be magical to wake up in his arms almost every morning, to kiss his lips even when things weren't going so well between us, and possibly to carry his baby in my belly.

"Good morning, Cogwyn. Do you want to stay for breakfast?" I asked him, noticing that he was still groggy after oversleeping. I did check the time on the clock on the wall and it said that it was already past ten in the morning.

We slept a lot because we were so tired last night. That was one of the many reasons why I convinced my Omega father that I wanted Cogwyn to sleep here.

He rubbed his eyes with his hands as he sat up on the bed. "Breakfast? Sure, love. I think I would like that."

Love? Wow.

I raked his body with my eyes as I said, "But first, I think you should get dressed."

He cracked open a smile, pushing the comforter away from his body as he got off the bed. I checked him out again as he went to where he had left his clothes, picked them up, and then put them on.

When he was finishing putting on his shirt and leather jacket, we heard someone rapping on the door. My eyes went wide when I realized it could only be a certain someone, and it was someone very important to me and very dear to my heart.

"Oh-oh," I said, going to the door and opening it. I wasn't surprised when I saw that it was my Omega father that had been rapping on the door. His eyes looked fierce and angry, like he was in the presence of something he despised so much he'd kill it if he could.

And by that I meant Cogwyn.

Ranulf glared over my right shoulder, finding the person he was looking for.

"I thought you had already left," he growled, stepping into the room and making his presence bigger than it was. Even though he was an Omega like I was, he was braver than most people thought he was. He thought he was just protecting me because he didn't think Cogwyn was the right man for me.

I knew why he was doing this and why he was thinking he was just protecting me, but I wasn't going to let him stand in the way of me and Cogwyn. Most of all, I wasn't going to let him sour this perfect moment I was sharing with him.

I leaped and stopped when I was in front of him, looking into his eyes as I realized he wasn't much taller than me.

"Could we just not do that now?" I begged him, hoping that he was going to understand me.

He sighed, saying, "Alright, I'm going to try to ignore him, and either way I came here for something else. We need to go and bury Parth, Bren. The police went there last night, picked up the bodies, and took them to the morgue."

I turned my head to look at Cogwyn, noticing that he was looking down. He was still also trying to process the news that his father was dead. I wished Ranulf could see what I was seeing, the pain in Cogwyn's eyes, and feel some empathy for him.

"And we should go there now after breakfast. They have some important news to tell us about the attack. They think they know why it happened."

As soon as he mentioned that, Cogwyn's eyes shot up. He hurried over to us, putting himself between me and Ranulf. "Did they tell you anything about it? Did they tell you why it happened?"

Ranulf narrowed his eyes and I could see that a vein in his neck was popping out. It didn't matter that he was much older than Cogwyn. He was still just an Omega like I was and, thus, he tended to be more submissive. He couldn't stand up to Cogwyn without going against what was in his nature.

He shook his head, responding, "No. Unfortunately, they didn't tell me anything." A tear broke out and rolled down his cheek. I could feel the pain he was feeling that his husband died. He wished he was there when it happened so that he could have stopped it. I doubted he would have been able to, but he still wished he was there.

Cogwyn tsked, striding to the door and marching into the hallway. As soon as I noticed it looked like he was going out, I went after him. He turned around, saying, "I don't think I have time for breakfast. Not today, anyway. Maybe some other time."

He turned around and strode out of the house, leaving me flabbergasted. I knew why he was in so much of a hurry. He wanted to make sure he was going to be there for his dead father in the morgue.

He wanted to make sure he was going to get what he needed as soon as possible because he had his vendetta to finish.

And thinking that, I couldn't help but feel that he was putting himself in danger when he didn't need to. I wanted revenge too, but he was alone in this.

Did I think that the other wolf shifters were going to help him with his vendetta? I didn't know, but I was going after him no matter what.

That's why, after glancing over my shoulder at my father, I took off after Cogwyn. I was going to stop him before he did something he'd regret later.

CHAPTER 10

Cogwyn

I was going to have my revenge and it didn't matter what happened from now on. First, I needed to go to the morgue to see my... dead father. I was just crossing out of the property when I heard footsteps coming from behind me hurriedly. I knew who they belonged to before I even turned around to see who it was.

As I turned around, I said, "Bren, I know we had an amazing night together, but I'm busy with something right now, and I think we should go to the morgue as soon as possible. Our fathers need us."

"I know that they do, but I want to go there with you."

Since waking up, I started to think about so many things. I started to think about what our relationship was going to lead to, the people that we were hurting because we were beginning to fall in love, and also that we were both pissing off our Omega fathers.

I knew what my other father thought of Bren and that he wasn't the right Omega for me. That was one of the many reasons why he didn't show up at the church.

I looked over his shoulder, noticing that his Omega father was staring at us from the doorway. He wished he could pull out a gun and shoot me dead right here, and he was not doing that because he didn't want to go to jail and make everything much worse.

I could feel the hatred he had for me and how it was swirling in the air. I could feel it in the way that it changed his scent, the way he kept his shoulders up and tense, and also the way his eyes were narrowed as he tried not to think about all the ways he could get rid of me.

I had a really amazing night with Bren and even though it was possible I got him pregnant, I couldn't help but wonder what our lives together would be like if he were to live with me.

He grabbed my hands, saying, "I'm going to end things with Ish and everything will be better. I want to stay with you."

As soon as he said that, I noticed his Omega father's shoulders pushing against his own body, like he was doing everything in his power not to spill out everything he was thinking right now.

I started to walk away, taking my hands off of his. "The more I stay in this place, the more I realize just how much your Omega father doesn't like me. He doesn't even feel sorry that my father was also killed in the attack."

Bren stopped in his tracks, exhaling. "I know he's having a hard time processing what happened, but he's a good person. I know that he'll come around one day, if you let him. Don't worry about him. Think about us."

I ran my hand over my face, thinking about my father and that I needed to find out what the police knew about the attack. I needed to find out everything they knew because I was going to use that information to finish my vendetta.

I just didn't have the time and the mind to think about our relationship right now, even though I knew very well that when we were making love and he was showing how much he wanted me, I promised myself I'd give ourselves a chance.

Well, that was then and things were different now.

I got on my bike when I realized that Bren was standing right by my side. I turned the handlebars of the motorcycle, firing up the engine.

"I'm going to the police station. If you want to come with me, you can, but I'm not going to stay another minute at your house. It's very clear to me that I'm not welcomed here at all."

"Aren't you at least going to try to call your friends to help you with this? I'm sure they want to get involved."

I thought about it, but I just didn't have the time to tell my boss about the attack and that I was still alive. Gosh, so many things happened between then and now I didn't even remember, this whole time, that I was part of a gang who prided themselves on how we always helped each other out.

"As soon as I get there, I'll tell them." I sighed, looking ahead at the road. When I turned my head to him, I said, "For your safety, I don't think you should come with me. The Bear Bikers might attack us again. I'm pretty sure that they are still trying to kill you."

When I was going to ride away on my bike, Bren grabbed my hand again and stopped me. He was looking into my eyes, which was something he never did often, as he said, "I should be going there with you anyway. My father is also very important to me and, if there is someone who I want to do this with, then it's you."

I sighed, saying, "But first, I need to go to the morgue, and then I'll go and get some support."

He smiled, swinging his leg over the bike as he sat down. When he wrapped his arms around my body, I already felt better. I could already imagine us riding in the streets, the wind blowing against our faces. It was like we were always meant to make this happen and be together.

His father came rushing to us right away, putting himself in front of the bike. "Where do you even think you are going with Bren?"

"To the morgue and don't worry – I'm going to bring him

back before the sun sets today."

He relaxed his shoulders, stepping away from the bike. "All right, but promise me that he'll be safe. I'm going to send some of my guards with you. They will follow you in their cars and make sure that you'll both be safe. I want to find out the truth about what happened as much as you do."

I nodded, realizing that we were finally agreeing on something. Hopefully, things were going to take a turn for the better between us. When I took off on my motorcycle, Bren buried his head in the crook of my neck as we went to the morgue.

He shifted his head slightly before asking, "Do you think we'll be okay together?"

"I'm sorry, what?" I asked, turning my head momentarily to glance at him.

He looked hurt by what I said, turning his head away.

Seconds later, when I realized he wasn't going to say anything else, I added, "What were you trying to say?"

He shook his head. "I don't think I want to talk about it anymore. You were so ready to leave me after we had that amazing night together."

"I'm not even sure what we are to each other anymore. I feel a strong pull to you, but I realize you're still much different than me and that we can't actually live together as a couple. I mean, are you going to want to live as a biker like me?" I asked him, studying his face to see what he thought about that.

"I was willing to do that, but it looks like you are the one who's not willing to change. I want to be with you for the rest of my life, even if that means fighting against the only father I still have."

I blinked twice, finding it hard to believe that he changed so much in so little time. Maybe it was his possible pregnancy that was changing him so much.

Either way, I didn't have time to think about building a family and having babies with him right now. I was aware that

I thought differently last night, but things changed and I just wanted my revenge as soon as possible.

CHAPTER 11

Bren

I thought that he was going to say to me we were going to build a family and that everything was going to be fine between us. The thing I had with Ish was nothing more than a fling, now that I was thinking better about it. I never really loved him. Not the way I loved this man who I was sure had knocked me up.

We walked out of the morgue and his biker friends were already standing outside, their motorcycles rumbling under the sunlight.

The leader was an older man with pepper and salt hair, a long beard, and a mean stare. Just looking at him now was making me feel afraid of him, even though I knew I didn't have to be. After all, he was part of us now. He was going to fight for us to help Cogwyn with his revenge.

And don't get me wrong when I say that I wanted revenge as well, but not in the way Cogwyn was thinking it should happen. He wanted revenge by his own hands and to teach the bear bikers that they should never have messed with him.

I was afraid of that because I didn't want him to put himself further in danger than he already was. But looking up and finding his eyes, I could tell that he wasn't about to change his mind. If anything, now that he saw his dead father in the morgue, he was even more determined about going through with his plan.

"I'm sorry about what happened," the president of the gang said, uncrossing his arms.

"I know, and I'm not letting things end this way. We need to get one of them and get all the information we need out of him, no matter the cost. They started a war with us as far as I'm concerned."

"I don't think I can change your mind about that and, don't worry, we'll make it happen. I'm just curious about one thing right now, though," the older man said, his intense eyes glaring at me like I was some kind of pestilence. I thought that that was going to be enough to make Cogwyn stand up for me and make me feel welcomed in his gang – even though I was pretty sure there was no way that was going to happen – but that's not what he did. His shoulders were still tense and I could tell he was still thinking about just one thing – killing all the people involved in the attack, and it didn't matter if that involved killing all of the bear bikers and continuing their war. "Why is here still with you? I thought that his kind didn't mingle with us bikers."

"He's here because his father was also killed. Our fathers thought that we were fated mates and were going to use the Sphere of Revelations to prove that. We didn't have enough time for that, though."

"I see," the president said, glancing me over with disdain in his eyes. If it was up to him, he'd be kicking me out of here right at this moment. But since Cogwyn was by my side and my father's bodyguards were with us, too, he wasn't going to do that.

But it was enough to make me feel even less welcomed in Cogwyn's world. He was right when he said that I wasn't going to become a biker and that I wasn't going to live like him.

And hell, if we were to have a child together, I didn't want him growing up in an environment that was about killing people and committing all kinds of other atrocities.

Even though Cogwyn was a better man than these people, our child would still be involved in all of that and I couldn't have that. We needed to have a definitive discussion about it and, hopefully, I could change his mind about it. But looking up and finding the eyes of the man who might have knocked me up – I still needed to wait until I could take the pregnancy test – I wasn't sure I wanted to have that conversation with him anytime soon.

It wasn't something that I could run away from, though, I thought.

"We'll see you in the club later, sharp. You know the time of the meeting. Be there and don't be late. We'll mount an attack, find out what's happening with the Bear Bikers, and hopefully figure out what's going on. Don't worry. We'll sort everything out."

Cogwyn nodded and the other bikers took off, turning to the right when they disappeared behind the buildings. I glanced at Cogwyn, wishing I could read his mind so that I could make all of this much easier.

I sighed and grabbed his hand to get his attention. It worked. He was looking at me, but it appeared he was determined about something that didn't involve our relationship. It looked like he was thinking about something else, focused just on it.

"Cogwyn…"

"What?"

"I think we need to talk about it, don't you?"

"About us?" He groaned, a car driving behind him.

"Yes, of course we need to talk about ourselves, or do you want to make me think that all that happened doesn't mean anything anymore to you?"

He ran his hand over his face, looking stressed out. "It was just a one-night stand. Just take a pill or something so that you don't get pregnant."

I didn't say anything, just letting silence take hold of the atmosphere between us. He wasn't looking directly at me, which was something new coming from him. Cogwyn always looked at my eyes when he was worried about something.

He wasn't doing this because he wanted to, was he?

"No, it was more than that. You shouldn't lie to me. I know it was more than that, and I know it means a lot that you can finally understand what's going on in my mind."

"I don't actually understand you that much," he growled, fur growing on his body. I didn't think he was going to transform, but it was more than evident that what was happening was making him feel more stressed.

"You do. When you were inside of me, I could understand you and you could understand me." I sighed, letting a moment of silence pass so that he could better understand what I meant by that.

"And I'm not going to take any pills. If I end up having your child, then I'll be happy to take care of him or her."

He widened his eyes, stepping toward me hurriedly. "You can't be serious about that. You can't have my child because we are not even fated mates. We'll never know that for sure."

Cogwyn was right about that, but we didn't need to know if we were fated mates or not. What the Sphere of Revelations was going to say didn't matter anymore. What mattered was what we felt about each other, and it was the strongest thing I felt right now.

"It's my choice, don't you think? I can do whatever I want. I'm just disappointed that you changed your mind about us all of a sudden. I thought we were building toward something more meaningful. I thought you were finally changing and becoming someone better than the asshole biker you were."

There. I said it. I just felt that it needed to be said. This whole time, Cogwyn was being an asshole again, almost like he was trying to toss me away after using me.

He blinked twice, stepping away from me as he went back to

his motorcycle. He grabbed the left handlebar as he said, "If I'm the asshole you think I am, then why do you still care about me?"

I stepped toward him, holding out a hand. It was like I was trying to reach out to him even though I knew it looked like he didn't want anything else to do with me. When I realized that, I lowered my hand and looked away. I hugged myself as I started to feel alone.

There was a moment of silence and, given the scent I could feel in the air, I was almost thinking he was beginning to regret the words he said to me.

"I hope you don't mean what you said. It hurt me more than I thought it would."

"Is there really no chance you could just drop your revenge and focus on building a life with me?" I asked, just wishing I could be holding his hand again.

He shook his head and didn't say anything. Moments later, he turned on the engine of the motorcycle and drove off, turning to the left when I couldn't see him anymore. I was left all alone on the sidewalk, wishing I could go back and reverse everything I said. I wished I could take it all back.

I turned and started to walk towards one of the cars that my bodyguards were driving. He opened the door and I sat down in the backseat, lowering my head and putting it on my hands. I was covering my face with my hands because I didn't want anyone to see it. I didn't want anyone to find out how much it hurt me. We just broke up even though we didn't even spend any time together, other than the night we shared in my bed.

And worse, the feeling that I got tossed away was growing stronger in my mind and it was beginning to make more sense than Cogwyn loving me.

Not to mention that if I was going to have his baby, then I was already beginning to feel happy that he or she would grow up in a much kinder environment, without the bikers and the violence that came with them.

"Do you want to go back home, master?" The bodyguard that was also the driver asked me, looking over his shoulder.

"Just take me wherever you want. I don't care anymore at this point," I barked, lying in the backseat as I wished I had someone to hold me tightly right now. I didn't just lose my father these last few days, but also the person who really connected with me in a way I had never felt before, which was one of the reasons why I now thought he was my fated mate.

The car was driving across the roads and I couldn't do anything that wasn't crying. If Cogwyn was still the same person I knew he was, he would be holding me in his arms right now and murmuring into my ear that everything was going to be fine. But it looked like I misjudged him. He went back to being his older self, who didn't care about anyone that wasn't himself...

◆ ◆ ◆

I felt a hand nudging my shoulder as I flapped my eyelids open, realizing that Ranulf had opened the door of the car and was standing by my side, outside the vehicle.

"I knew he was going to leave you. I tried to warn you, but he was just using you. He's always been like that. Don't you remember anymore all the times when you came home from school crying because of him?" He asked when I sat up in the backseat, looking at his comforting eyes.

I nodded, saying, "You're right. You've always been right and I'm sorry I said the things I said to you."

As I got out of the car and the driver took it to the garage, Ranulf asked, "You didn't have sex with him when he was in your room, right?"

I knew why he was asking about that. He was worried I was pregnant with Cogwyn's baby.

I just shook my head and said, "No, it didn't happen. He just slept in my room, but he slept on the floor."

Ranulf studied my face for a fraction of a second, looking

away as we crossed the main door into the main hall.

"Good. That means we don't have to worry about it."

CHAPTER 12

Cogwyn

Months later, I was still thinking about everything that happened. I left Bren because I couldn't stand his father, the environment where he lived, and all the people in his life who always thought so highly of themselves.

I was on my motorcycle, waiting for a certain asshole to show up. He was one of the Bear Bikers, stumbling out of the bar as he loosely held a bottle of beer. One of the other customers of the place kicked him out, shouting, "Get out of here and never come back."

He was so drunk he couldn't even finish his transformation. His irises changed their color, his nails popped out, but then, seconds later, he was already fully back to his human form.

I couldn't help but chuckle, getting off Desire and stepping toward him, measuring the weight of my footsteps because I didn't want to alert anyone about my presence. I was deep in Bear territory and if they got a whiff of me, there would be hell. I was doing this alone because more people involved in this assignment would only make things worse.

Not to mention that I needed to do this on my own anyway. The president and the rest of the Wolf Shifters were doing all they could – or at least they were trying to make me think they were – regarding the murder of my father, but I was pretty sure they could still be doing more. I was just disappointed in them was all.

I took the left when he entered an alleyway. The poor guy didn't even know where he was going, bouncing off a wall as he lost his balance and fell over on the ground. I was just behind him and I was going to do everything in my power to get as much information out of him as I could.

I knew the names of the people behind the attack and I was going to kill them, one by one. My fur was growing back on my skin as I tried to suppress my scent. I couldn't let the guy I was pursuing find out that I was coming for him, or any of the people who lived here in this neighborhood, for that matter. I didn't want more attention on me than I already had.

He turned his head to look behind his shoulder when he felt a presence looming behind him. "Who the hell are you and what are you doing here? You don't look like someone from the family," he said, crawling away from me.

"No, I don't, and I'm here for you and not for them. Do you remember Misk Garrett, the CEO of Wolfza?" I growled, hoping that my voice and the tone I was using were going to make him piss his pants.

"No, who's he?" He asked, his voice sounding slow, and it annoyed me every time he spoke. I grabbed him by the collar of his shirt and hoisted him, noticing that my nails were growing. I needed to control my transformation or else my scent was going to give away that I was here.

I studied his eyes, realizing that he was speaking the truth when he said that. He was just a low-level grunt of the gang and it was likely that he didn't even know what he was doing when he attacked me and my family.

"Think better about it. Think very carefully about that night when you tried to kill me." I stared into his eyes, giving him time to remember my face. When his eyes bulged, I knew that I finally had him where I wanted him.

"You are Cogwyn Garrett. We should've killed you when we had the chance. My life turned into a living hell because of you."

Knowing that he was suffering because of me and the Wolf shifters was empowering. I took pleasure in that and I wasn't going to hide it, a smile showing up on my face.

"Good. You should be afraid of me and you should always remember my name and face." I shoved him against the wall of a building and he almost lost his consciousness, his eyes closing until I punched him against the wall again. "I want you to tell me everything you did that night. I want you to tell me why you attacked us. My father never did anything against you. He was just a businessman."

He turned his eyes slowly as he stared at me again. "I don't think I should tell you anything. You won't let me get out of this alive even if I do."

I felt my body growing bigger, my muscles straining against my clothes.

"Thing is, I don't think you have a choice. You either get a chance at escaping this by telling me everything you know, or I kill you right now and find someone else to extract the information I need."

He whimpered, throwing his beer bottle against me, but I slapped it away. It exploded on the ground into a million pieces, beer splashing out of it.

I shoved him against the wall again, my nails growing bigger as my skin started to be covered by my fur.

"Tell me everything you know. I'm not going to give you another chance."

"Alright, alright," he mumbled, taking a deep breath. "But if you think that you're going to like my answer and what I know, you'll be disappointed."

"Why is that?" I growled, wishing I could open a hole in his neck. I was going to do that as soon as I didn't need him anymore.

Thing was, I needed him now because he was the only idiot in the Bear Bikers who was alone sometimes. All the others always walked in groups and they also never got wasted like this guy was.

"I remember that you were in a relationship with a certain Omega by the name of Bren..."

I blinked, not understanding why he mentioned Bren all of a sudden. I was surprised that a guy like him knew about the beginning of a relationship that never really flourished.

"What do you know about him?" I asked, feeling that even after all this time, the mere mention of his name was enough to make me feel stressed out about the way things turned out.

"It was his father who ordered the attack. Your Omega fathers did. They never wanted you together. That's what happened."

When he said that, I eased my grip and he fell to the floor, scurrying away as soon as he could. I was paralyzed by his words and I had no reason to believe he lied. My Omega father and Bren's ordered the attack against us? It didn't even make any sense. Even though they knew each other, they never really talked.

When I turned my head to try and find that drunkard again, he was already gone and I was alone in the alleyway. I heard police sirens in the distance and I didn't think that they were coming this way.

Still, I decided to move away from there as fast as I could as I went back to Desire. I swung my leg over the motorcycle, turned on the engine, and started to ride away from there.

When I was out of the Bear Bikers' territory, I could finally try to process what I knew. If my Omega father was one of the parties who ordered the attack, then I needed to have a straight conversation with him.

I needed to look into his eyes to find out the truth. And then, I'd need to also talk to Ranulf and find out if I could dig out the rest of the truth.

The motorcycle screeched to a halt and I jumped off of it, storming into my apartment room. I was still trying to process everything that he said to me, my mind remembering the amazing night I had with Bren. Truth was, even after breaking up with him, he was always in my mind. I always thought of him, even when things were going well in my life.

Could it be that he really was my fated mate? I didn't know, but he still meant a lot to me and I had no idea if he got pregnant or not. We never talked again after we 'broke up.'

My mind was such a mess and now I needed to go and find out the truth about what happened.

CHAPTER 13

Bren

I was walking down the sidewalk when I started to hear the rumbling of a motorcycle's engine. I didn't think much of it, knowing that I lived in a city where bikers were everywhere. My hands were in my pockets, my head lowered.

Since breaking up with Cogwyn and then Ish, I hadn't been the same person. I tried pushing all the bad memories out of my mind, but I always kept thinking that something was wrong with me, especially after finding out that I was pregnant.

My belly was big now, but I knew it was going to grow even bigger. I put my hands on it, sliding them on it as I continued to walk across the sidewalk. I kept on ignoring the sound of the motorcycle's engine as I knew it couldn't be Cogwyn.

He left his mark on me and it was always going to be there.

I could still remember the night when he took my virginity and made me his. But the next day, he was already spouting out a lot of bullshit that we weren't going to work as a couple, that we should live separately, and that my life was better without him.

I shook my head, hating the fact that he said those things to me and I wasn't able to rebuke him. I was still trying to process everything that happened then.

I turned my head to the left when I heard the motorcycle pulling over. For a moment, I thought that it was a thug trying to rob me, but it was just a biker with his girlfriend, who was in the backseat. It looked like she was an Omega like I was, and I had to say that the biker was hot himself.

I stopped walking just to admire them, but I immediately went back to what I was doing because I didn't want to come off as a creep.

I turned to the left, crossed the crosswalk, and then went toward where the bar I was looking for was. It was a dive bar located in the neighborhood where my house was, and from the reviews I saw on the Internet, it appeared to be good.

I heard a couple of rumbles sounding from the clouds in the sky and I looked up as I realized that it looked like there was going to be a rainstorm in the city soon.

I lowered my eyes when I realized that another motorcycle was pulling over, this time much closer to me. When I turned my head to see who was doing that, my jaw dropped when I realized it was none other than the guy who dumped me when I most needed him.

Cogwyn, and he looked just like I remembered him, looking at me as if he had something very important to say to me. I froze up where I was, not understanding anymore what was happening. After all these months, when I couldn't even hide my pregnancy by putting on a sweater, he decided to show up?

To say that I was furious would be an understatement and a huge one at that.

Remembering the last words he said to me, I marched up to him. When he got off the bike, I shoved my finger against his chest.

"What are you doing here? Why did you come looking for me?" I stared into his eyes, which was something I stopped doing often. "Did you come here to see how fucked up I am because of you?"

He exhaled, grabbing my hand and moving it away from his chest.

"I didn't come here to mock or make fun of you," he explained, letting go of my hand when he realized I wasn't going to hit him. "I came here because I just learned who ordered the attack against us. Everything finally makes sense."

I took a step away from him, my eyes bulging wide.

"After all this time, after leaving me pregnant, the first thing you say is that you found out about who was behind it?" My eyes checked him out from bottom to top, almost like I was wishing he was nothing more than a ghost. "And the fact I am pregnant – does it mean nothing to you?"

His eyes went down, finally noticing my belly. I was surprised that it took him this long to realize I was pregnant. He was the only and first person I had sex with, so the baby had to be his.

He hurried over to me with semi-open arms. He was trying to show me he was surprised by the fact I was pregnant, that it was huge news to him, but I wasn't going to have any of that.

I put my hand against his chest and shoved him away from me.

"Stay away from me! Stay away from me and my son." I felt a tear coming out and rolling down my cheek. "You've ruined my life. I even considered killing myself because of you."

His facial features softened and he lowered his arms.

"Look, I'm really sorry about everything that happened, but I didn't think that contacting you after we broke up was a good idea, so I decided not to do it." He held my gaze, his eyes filled with something I didn't want to admit was there. "I should've asked you, at least, if you were okay."

I crossed my arms over my chest. "Yeah, you should've done that. There were a lot of things you should've done."

After a moment of silence, he moved his hand so that it was pointing at a bench not too far from us.

"Do you want to sit down with me so that we can talk about it?" When he realized I wasn't going to respond, he added, "And it's really such a nice surprise to know that you're pregnant with my baby. We might not be fated mates, but it's good to know that I'm a father now."

Perhaps it was my Omega instincts that were driving me to go there with him, but either way, we went there. I sat down on it and he was by my side, his hands clasped between his legs.

"I suppose there's nothing I can do to make things better, right?" He asked, looking at my eyes and trying to find out if there was something he could say to make me forgive him.

I shook my head. It was a tough pill for him to swallow, but I knew he could.

"Alright, so let's put behind what I came here for and talk about this," he pointed with both of his hands to my pregnant belly. "You really never thought about calling me to tell me about it this whole time?"

"How was I going to do that when I don't even have your number and you are pretty much someone who doesn't exist on the Internet?"

He nodded, biting his bottom lip. I was right. How was I going to contact someone who was always trying to make himself as invisible as possible from the Internet?

"Then, I just want to say that I'm happy I finally know I'm going to become a father. It's the best news I've had all day."

I examined his eyes, trying to find out if he was telling me the truth or not. It looked like he was, which was a big plus for him. I thought he was just going to look over the fact he put a baby in my belly, but it was the opposite that was happening.

He looked exuberant that he was going to become a dad, even though I had no idea if we would ever live together and if he would have a presence in my baby's life.

I did, however, feel a little closer to him now that he said he was thrilled he was going to become a father.

"And it doesn't matter if you ever forgive me or not – I'm still going to do everything in my power to help the baby and you."

How could my heart fight against someone who was looking

so regretful about what he did? Cogwyn wasn't using the exact words I was looking for, but he was still saying he made a mistake when he dumped me and went to do whatever he went to do that time.

His eyes were shimmering with happiness and hope. Cogwyn hoped he could turn my mind around about the fact I didn't like him anymore.

CHAPTER 14

Cogwyn

It was the hugest news all day the fact that Bren was pregnant. I didn't forget about the night we had and I always wondered if he had gotten pregnant, but I didn't contact him to ask if he was feeling better and so, this whole time, I had no idea he was carrying my baby in his belly.

Even though we were never going to find out if the Sphere of Revelations was going to say we were fated mates, everything was happening as if we were.

All I knew was that I couldn't walk away from this. This Omega was pregnant with my baby and I was hoping I could change his mind about what he thought of me. I wanted to bond with him again, to become his Alpha like I was at that time. That time… I was still talking about it like it happened years ago.

I grabbed his hand even though I knew he wasn't going to like it. I thought he was going to pull it back right away, but he didn't do that. He let me caress his hand like we were lovers again.

Tears were rolling down his cheeks and I wished I could dry them with my hands. I needed to do this slowly so that he wasn't spooked.

I was brushing my finger over his hand as I said, "I'm going to do everything for the baby. I'll bust my ass off and buy him everything he needs, and I don't care if he's an Alpha or an Omega, or even a Beta."

The reason why I was saying that was because Betas were looked down upon in our society. People thought that they were outcasts and shouldn't be a part of society.

The reason behind that was pretty simple. Alphas and Omegas formed the perfect pairs and Betas were the middle-ground between us, not being one or the other, and usually preferring hooking up with themselves than with us.

That's one of the reasons why most of the Bear Bikers were Betas and not Alphas. They thought they were inferior to us. They couldn't fit in.

"Ah, fuck it," Bren said all of a sudden, making me wonder what was going on in his mind, but that was only for half of a second. A moment later, he was interlacing his arms around my neck, pulling me to him for a hot kiss.

I couldn't take my lips off of him and I didn't think he wanted me to do that anyway. If anything, he'd always been looking forward to doing this with me and had always wondered what it would be like to kiss me again.

I dug my tongue into his mouth, drilling it in for a short battle. Bren moaned into my mouth and I threw my arms around his body, putting my hand on the back of his head.

As our lips brushed against each other, I couldn't help but feel hard, remembering that time when I penetrated him and everything was better. I was inside of him and I felt like my life was complete. I was wondering if I could do things right this time or if it was hopeless and he was only kissing me now so that he could get his revenge.

After all, Bren had always been a guy who wasn't beyond petty acts of revenge. It would hurt me quite a lot if he was doing this now only to make me think there was some hope for us when, in fact, there wasn't.

He pulled his head back suddenly, regarding me with shimmering eyes.

"Wait, what the hell was that?" I groaned, refusing to move my arms away from him.

"You looked like such a proper daddy for our son that I couldn't resist it."

"Huh?"

"Just shut up and kiss me again," he groaned, pulling me for another hot kiss, my cheeks pressing against his and feeling the wetness of his tears. I never thought I'd ever see someone so snobby being so hungry to kiss me again and again.

I pressed my lips against his lips, moving my hands over his shoulders as I kneaded his skin. I could even feel the beating of his heart and the warmth rising to my cheeks. I could feel my eyes transforming, becoming more like those of a wolf.

I couldn't resist my transformation, knowing that Bren really was the right person for me – the one I had been looking for, this whole time, even though I didn't think that was the case.

Our lips were wet and hot, his breathing quickening. I pulled my head back and settled my hand on his cheek, moving it around and around.

"Uh, wow, that was the best kiss I had in a long time."

"Don't tell me you kissed other guys when I wasn't around."

"No, I didn't," I affirmed, remembering that I had been far too focused on finding out the truth about the attack instead. I had eyes just for him since then, and it made sense that I couldn't find someone who could stir the same kind of fire within me.

I was having difficulty with breathing too, thinking about just one thing right now – taking him to my bed. I couldn't take him to his house. What that Bear Biker asshole told me had to have been right.

It was our Omega fathers who had ordered that hit against us. They thought that us being fated mates would disown their families and bring destruction to their legacies or some bullshit like that.

To be honest, just thinking about it right now was making my stomach churn. Even if it made sense and I had to face my Omega dad about it, I just wanted to pretend I didn't have anything to do with it.

"Good," he purred, pulling me up and taking me to my motorcycle. Why was he doing that? I knew he didn't like Desire.

Well, I supposed it was his love for me that was speaking louder than anything else in his mind that was making him do this right now. "I really think we're made for each other."

"I think the same way," I said, getting back on my bike and putting him in the backseat.

After he wrapped his arms around my torso, he said, "Take me to my home. I want to do this with you there again."

I bit my bottom lip, feeling a little bad that I couldn't grant him his wish.

"There was also something very important I needed to tell you. It's about our Omega fathers..."

I was going to continue my explanation when he covered my mouth with his hand.

"Let's not talk about them right now. I'm okay if you don't want to take me to my home, but please find us a private place where I can feel comfortable with you."

I smiled, tucking those horrible thoughts where they weren't going to be a bother to me.

"That I can do," I purred, riding off on the motorcycle toward my apartment. We crossed through several streets before getting there and I kicked the door open when we arrived.

I was holding him in my arms, wishing we had a better place to do this. My dick was so hard in my pants that it was pushing up against them. I started to pepper his neck with several kisses, loving the feel of his skin against my lips.

"You are my love. I thought I could stop thinking about you after we broke up, but in the end, I was wrong about that as well," I admitted, holding his gaze for what appeared to be an eternity.

"Something about that tells me I knew it was always going to happen," he murmured when I put him down on my bed. A moment later, I climbed up on top of him.

When I lowered my head so that I was devouring his neck with my lips, he started to squirm and say over and over again how much he needed me.

The way he was saying that was making me feel even more turned on than I was before, my shaft hard and leaking my pre-come.

"Say it to me how much you love me," I demanded of him, my hands groping his body and feeling every one of his curves. And they were just perfect, his body begging for me to be inside of him right now.

"I love you more than any other person in the world," he groaned, answering me. The way he said that made me feel like ripping the clothes off of his body, which I did a moment later.

When he was naked and breathing hard, sweat pooling on his forehead and in his armpits, I knew that the moment I had been waiting for since our breakup was finally happening, and I was a much happier man for it.

CHAPTER 15

Bren

I didn't think it was going to happen, but when Cogwyn was saying those sweet things to me and how he was promising me he was going to try to be a good father to our son, no matter what I said, I couldn't resist it and so I kissed him.

We connected our lips and since then I couldn't stop thinking about him, even though most of that was because he was right on top of me, grinding his body against me over and over.

I was a little bigger now and heavier, my belly rubbing against his abs, but it was okay. Cogwyn was still the same ruthless guy I knew he was, but he was being more careful with me this time.

He roamed his hands over my body, stopping when they were underneath my asscheeks. He squeezed them, moving down over the bed as he put his tongue out of his mouth and started to lick my junk. I groaned and grabbed his hair, pulling him down further so that he was all over my shaft and balls, his lips so hungry for more.

Meanwhile, I was thinking about the life we were going to have together, not even remembering the fact that he mentioned something about our Omega fathers and how they were involved in something I had no idea about.

"Gosh, this is almost too much," I moaned, putting my hands

on his back and digging my fingers into his skin. His body was a little slick thanks to his sweat, which I was loving. The sweat was making our bodies wetter, pre-come coming out through my slit.

"Tell me if you need a moment to catch your breath," he groaned into my ear as he turned me around so that I was on all fours on the bed. My body was shivering. I was worried he was going to penetrate me and fuck me even though I was already pregnant. I didn't want to do anything that could hurt the baby.

He inched closer to me, his body touching mine and engulfing it.

When he neared his mouth to my ear again, I knew that he was going to say something about that.

"Don't worry – I'm going to be kind, just like last time."

And I knew he was going to be, even though it wasn't going to make things any easier for me. As he grabbed my ass and pulled me to him, I felt his dick nudging my entrance. Cogwyn was torturing me by teasing me and even though he knew how evil that was, he was smiling as he showed me how much he was enjoying this.

"I know you're going to," I purred, thrusting my ass against his dick as I felt the need for him to be inside of me right away.

When he was through the first barrier and then was lodged inside of me, I felt like stars were exploding in my mind.

This beast of a man, who was already turning and becoming more like a wolf, was going to knot me and become one with me. He moved his hands around my body as he put them on my belly, caressing it.

"I'm just so happy I'm going to be a father," he said as he started to thrust in and out, his pace slow in the beginning. It was almost too slow and even though I thought that way about it, I was still enjoying it.

I even put my legs over his shoulders so that I was even closer to him than I should be.

When he picked up his pace, I was sad that it meant we were almost done. His balls started to slap against my asscheeks, his body becoming one with mine just like I thought it was going to be.

He locked his eyes with me as his dick grew inside of me, knotting me. Moments later, it was throbbing and erupting inside my tunnel, painting it in white with his come. I closed my eyes and came at the same time, my body rocking and convulsing.

Moments later, I reopened my eyes and all I could see was his face. His eyes were shimmering with happiness and love, and I knew how much it meant to him that we were doing this.

His dick was still so big inside of me.

"Holy shit, that was incredible," I moaned, my hands grabbing his shoulders because I didn't want to feel like I wasn't doing enough. This was incredible. It was the second time I was having sex in my life and it was almost as good as the first time. The only thing I regretted about it was that I wasn't going to get pregnant again.

"I'm ready to do more of this with you when you want to, my love," he murmured into my ear, kissing the side of my neck as he made me squirm against his massive body.

I cracked open a gentle smile as I read his eyes and I knew he was telling the truth.

Seconds later, and I said this as I felt a little sad about it, his dick started to return to its normal shape as I knew we were reaching the end of it.

I wished we could do just one more thing to make tonight more special, almost like it was our wedding night and it was supposed to be a moment that should forever be in our minds.

He pulled out of me when I was parting my lips to say to him what was in my mind.

He brushed his hand over my cheek as he finally realized I had a dirty, little proposition for him.

"Something on your mind?" He asked, his eyes gleaming under the moonlight coming through the windows.

"I want to feel you inside of me again."

He curled up the side of his lips, saying, "But you just did. I knew you were always hungry for me, but I never thought you were so insatiable."

"It's way more than that. There's something I just never did with you."

He widened his eyes slightly as he showed confusion.

He was just opening his mouth when I pushed him against the bed, putting myself right over his dick. It was already semi-hard, but if I worked on it long enough, I was pretty sure I could make it hard again.

"What are you doing-" he groaned as I wrapped my lips around his cockhead and started to suck on it, swirling my tongue under the underside of it, making him throw his head backward.

I took my mouth off of his dick just to say, "Do you like it?" When I smacked my lips, I felt that they were sticky with his pre-come. "I myself am enjoying this very much."

"You're naughtier than I thought you were," he said as he smiled gently. I was all over his dickhead again, swirling my tongue around it and suckling on it. He was so tasty and salty, which was just the way I liked it.

He drew in a short breath as he grabbed my hair and thrust my head down, making me deepthroat him. It came out of nowhere and I was surprised by it, but I wasn't shocked. I wasn't going to say I had any experience deep-throating a man, but I was already getting used to it.

He was so deep inside of my mouth and throat that I couldn't even use my tongue the way I wanted to. Nevertheless, I could feel that he was enjoying this, his breathing quickening as I knew he was close to climaxing again.

"I'm only going to stop this when you're coming inside my

mouth," I said after taking my mouth off of his cock.

"I can't wait for that, then," he joked, and I went back to where I was, deep-throating him as much as I could until he was climaxing inside my mouth, his dick shaking and convulsing like it was a trapped beast.

I pulled my head back and kissed his cockhead, loving the way his hands were groping my body as he showed me he still hadn't had enough of me.

I plopped down on the bed as I hugged him and buried my body in his arms. I could even hear his heart beating in his chest, my lips already looking for his lips because I needed one more thing to feel connected to him.

CHAPTER 16

Cogwyn

I woke up and wondered what I was going to get us to eat in the morning. Snowflakes were falling from the sky outside and I could tell that it was already winter – or at least, I was remembering that it was.

My mind had been so worried about that revelation about the attack that I hadn't even stopped to think about the weather and what my days were like. All I knew was that I was getting stressed out over little things that didn't matter at all.

He was still in my arms, his body snuggled up in mine. I just wanted to hold him in my arms like this for the rest of my life, even though I knew it wasn't possible.

That day outside looked beautiful and I just wanted to go there and play in the snow with him.

I was just turning my head to look back at him when I realized he was opening his eyes again. Seconds later, Bren was looking at me and wondering what I was thinking.

"Is it morning already?" He asked, sounding lazy.

"It is, but you don't need to get off the bed if you don't want to."

And I was still trying to come up with the right way to tell him that we were going to go for takeout because I didn't have anything in the kitchen. I didn't have food, utensils, and pretty much everything else I needed to make a proper breakfast for him.

I was caressing his cheek when I said, "It's snowing outside."

"It is?" He asked, sounding lazy as he kept his head on my chest. "I had no idea we were even in the Winter season already. I thought it was Fall."

"I'm just as surprised as you are."

Meanwhile, I was wondering how I was going to approach the subject of his father being one of the culprits who ordered the attack. I know that it was a very delicate subject and I didn't want to ruin this perfect morning we were having.

Minutes passed and we didn't do anything. When I checked the clock on the side table, I realized that it was already ten in the morning and that his stomach was rumbling.

"Hungry? I guess you're going to be disappointed. I can't cook."

That was something about me I tried to hide from him, until now. I'd never cooked in my life. I never had to, after all.

"Really?" He asked, making me feel worried that I was going to lose him again because I was disappointing him. But then, he smiled gently. "I also don't know how to cook, so if we live together we'll certainly have to hire someone to fill that role."

I smiled back at him, sat up on the bed, and then got off of it. I was naked and I noticed that he was checking me out as I started to put my clothes on.

It was like we never broke up and had always been together. Things were developing so quickly since he reappeared in my life that it was kind of scary. But it was scary in a good way, too.

When I was turning around, Bren got off the bed and put on his clothes. I looked at his belly, wondering how many months he had left until the baby was born.

We went outside and I took him to one of his favorite restaurants. No takeout. I was lying when I said we were going to go for takeout. We didn't have much money, especially because his

Omega father kept most of their money for himself, but we had enough for breakfast.

We were just walking out of the restaurant when I put my hand on his shoulder and guided him to one of the alleyways, where we had the privacy we needed to talk about something important.

"The food was delicious," he purred, connecting his lips against my mouth again.

"I'm glad you liked it," I said, feeling sad that our breakfast was already over. I wished that nothing could be changed, living this dream with him for the rest of my life, but the truth was that I couldn't hide from it. "But... I need to go back to what I was going to say to you when I found you."

His body became tense all of a sudden, eyes trembling.

"Can't we just forget it entirely? Can't we just forget the city, our families, and just go and live somewhere else where none of those things can bother us?"

I sighed, realizing just how important that was to him. It would be nice if we could make that happen, but things weren't like in the movies. We needed to face the truth before it crashed against us.

"Unfortunately, my love, we can't," I said.

"I was really afraid of this," he said, lowering his head while I refused to move my hands away from his shoulders. I just wanted to be as close to him as I could be.

I took a deep breath in before I finally said, "Our Omega fathers... They were the ones who ordered the attack. They don't want us together. They thought we could never know that we really are fated mates, just like that foreseer told us."

He snapped his head back up, his eyes locking with mine.

"You're kidding, right? Please tell me you are. It doesn't make any sense."

"Love, I know that it doesn't make sense, but I did some digging and... It's true. You believe me, right?"

He shook his head, stepping away from me even though I had my hands on his shoulders.

"It just can't be possible. This can't be happening. I know Ranulf and I know that he would never do anything that could harm his husband. They were in love. They always said they'd always do anything for each other."

"I know you are having difficulty believing me about it, but why would I lie? I love my Omega father as well. I'm just as disappointed and angry as you are."

He whirled around, his eyes locking with my eyes again. They studied my expression as he tried to find out what I was thinking. When he realized I really wasn't lying or was hiding part of the truth, he succumbed to his knees.

I went to him right away, putting my arms around him as he started to sob and cry.

"I'm really sorry about it."

He was still crying on my shoulder when he said, "Ranulf tried to kill us. I just can't believe it. I need to confront him and tell the police what we know."

"I don't think we should tell the police about it."

He pulled his head back, looking at me with disbelief in his eyes.

"Why not? They'll be able to confirm your information and do what they need to do. After all, this whole time, they haven't been able to do anything worthwhile for the case."

"I just don't trust them. Not to mention that, when they see it's a biker telling them that, the first thing they'll do is to ignore what I know."

He exhaled and stood up with me. We went back to Desire and I put him on the backseat, feeling his arms wrapping around my torso.

"I understand. So, what do you think we should do?"

"I need to sneak up into my father's room and find out if there's anything there I can use against him. After all, we need solid proof that he did what we know."

And it was going to be somewhat easy to do that. He still had no idea that I knew what I knew. It was just going to be a little more difficult to get into the house. After all, I hadn't gone there in a very long time - ever since they kicked me out because I wanted to become a biker.

"I'm going to find out everything I can in my father's office and his room."

I snapped my head to look over my shoulder and find his trembling eyes. "No, you don't need to do that. Leave it to me. I don't want you risking yourself and our little one."

He cracked open a smile, shaking his head. "Don't worry. I'm not going to do anything I haven't already done. After all, how many times do you think I entered his room when he locked it from me?"

I knew he felt confident about it, but I still couldn't help but worry about him.

CHAPTER 17

Bren

Opening the door, I still found myself in Ranulf's room. I looked behind my shoulder and I didn't see him or hear him coming anywhere near here. The house was quite silent in this cold and snowy morning, snowflakes falling outside.

Alright, I was here in his room and I could see he had left many memories of his marriage to my Alpha father. Their portraits together, pictures, trophies, mementos, and that sort of stuff dotted the room, and it all made me think that Cogwyn's information had to be wrong.

Perhaps it was more like a suspicion than the truth... I was kind of hoping it was so that we could focus on the most important thing at hand and find the true culprits. That would be much easier than knowing it was my father's husband the one who ordered his death.

Or perhaps something happened in the attack that he couldn't quite tell me about? Maybe something went wrong? I didn't know, but I was curious.

I peeked over my shoulder when I thought I heard a pair of footsteps approaching the door. Ranulf didn't know this about me, but I was quite good at sneaking around and opening doors. He was probably still thinking that I was in my room, brooding about the fact I was pregnant and didn't know what was happening to Cogwyn.

The door to the room was closed. I'd hear him opening it before he had the chance to find out that I was here. I wasn't going to leave his things where they weren't before. I was going to be meticulous in my search.

Hopefully, this wasn't going to take too long, either.

I went to his desk, opened the top drawer, and I wasn't surprised when I found only paper sheets after paper sheets detailing his business decisions. He worked home office for a multinational company, in their PR department, and thus there wasn't anything worthwhile here.

I'd once considered working a similar job as him, but then I realized it wasn't for me. I didn't look it, but I was thinking about becoming a PE teacher. So many of my high school teachers said I had the natural attributes to become one.

Opening another drawer, I wasn't surprised when I still didn't find what I came here for. I mean, did I think I really was going to find the information I needed in his office?

The police had already finished a thorough search of the place and didn't find anything. They didn't think he was one of the perpetrators, but they still needed to do that because it was part of their operation.

I pressed my hand against my back, feeling the weight of the belly. I moved my hand over it in small circles as I thought more and more about the life I was thinking about having with my... husband.

I chuckled. Thinking that way about Cogwyn was something I'd thought would never happen, but here I was, thinking that nothing else could feel righter than that.

I opened a couple more drawers, looked behind the books in his bookshelves, under the bed, and pretty much everywhere else I could think of, only to realize I was probably out of luck.

I stood up and was turning around when I realized that the

door was already open and in front of it was standing the man who I had even stopped thinking about. It wasn't that I forgot about him, but that I didn't think he was going to show up so soon – and especially without my knowing about it.

I froze up. It was too late. Ranulf knew that I was in his room without his knowledge and okay, and he looked pretty disappointed that I went behind his back.

He clasped his hands behind his back, coming toward me. His footsteps were composed and controlled, almost like he was doing everything in his power not to lash out at me right now.

"I was looking for something."

A moment of silence when he stopped walking, standing a couple of feet across from me. "Are you going to tell me why, or do I have to take that information out of you?"

"Cogwyn said you were the one who ordered the attack against us. You killed your own husband."

He widened his eyes. "I'm surprised that you are back together again. Or maybe I shouldn't be. Someone told me that he saw you with him in a rundown apartment building in the middle of nowhere. You disappointed me more by doing that than sneaking into my room and looking through my stuff."

"He also said that you ordered the attack because you didn't like that we are fated mates, just like that foreseer said we are. The Sphere of Revelations…"

"Yes, it was going to confirm it and I couldn't have it."

I widened my eyes, finding it unbelievable that he was confirming everything to me without giving it a second thought. His expression was so serene I couldn't even try reading what he was thinking right now.

"You're being far too calm about this. Are you thinking about killing me here as well? I looked up to you when I was growing up."

"And you stopped being like that when you met Cogwyn for the first time. He started to change you. You became more rebellious because of him, fighting me and Parth because you had such a huge crush on him you couldn't control yourself..."

"The fact I had a crush on him didn't change anything about me."

"How not?" He asked, curling up the corner of his lips. He lifted his right hand as he pointed it to me and said, "You've gotten pregnant and I know that he's the father. He's the only person you ever had sex with."

I blushed. "I didn't think you were keeping tabs on that. I thought that my personal life was just that."

"It is and I care about you – more so than you think I do. There's a good reason why I didn't want you two together."

I didn't say anything for the next minute or so, holding his gaze for as long as I could.

"So, you're really confirming that you were behind the attack. You betrayed the Wolf Shifters by asking those Bear Bikers to come after us."

A tear broke out and rolled down his cheek.

"You know, I really loved your father. Parth was everything to me, but then cracks started to show up in our married life, and we didn't know how to deal with them. He was even thinking about sleeping in a separate room. Of course, it didn't end up happening because he didn't have enough time, but he said he was thinking about it."

"I hope that wasn't enough reason for you to kill him. He didn't deserve it."

"I wasn't the one who came up with the plan."

I widened my eyes, surprised more than anything that he was finally confirming what I came here for. It turned out that I wasn't going to need solid proof to confront him about it.

I was already recording this conversation and I was going to give it to the police so that they could lock him up.

"I'm disappointed in you. I actually came here looking for proof that you didn't do what Cogwyn accused you of."

"No, he's partially right. It was Eleric the one who came with the crazy plan to attack you when you were in the church. I tried to convince him to change his mind, but it was too late. He was already hell-bent on getting rid of both of you.

I did say that he shouldn't kill our husbands, that only Cogwyn had to die, but of course, the Bear Bikers fucked it up."

I took a step backward. He just said that they were only supposed to kill my lover and spare everyone else. I thought that they were supposed to kill all of us.

He took a step toward me when his eyes went down and he realized that my phone was in the pocket of my pants.

He leaped toward me, trying to grab it out of my pocket, but then I turned around quickly and started to race out of the house. I needed to get to Cogwyn as fast as possible and before Ranulf had enough time to order his bodyguards to grab me.

I needed to transfer the recording to Cogwyn's phone. When he had it and also the evidence he was looking for in his former house, he would then have enough to put our Omega fathers behind bars.

I was just going out of the property when I felt his hand grabbing my shoulder, and then he yanked me to him with enough force to make me fall over on my ass.

When I looked up, I realized that I had fucked things beyond repair.

CHAPTER 18

Cogwyn

"I can't believe you did what you did," I said, growling as I felt my canines growing. I was growing bigger, my body beginning to press against my clothes. I didn't want to turn and become a wolf in front of my Omega father, but the way he was looking at me with such disdain on his face was infuriating.

I thought that I was going to come here and find out I was wrong about it, but when he realized that I was coming back home after years of being away from it, he decided to reveal everything and speak to me like he knew he would never be locked up for his crime.

"If you came here really looking for information that I wasn't involved in the attack, then you were a fool. I was one of the few who knew about what was going to happen in the church. I didn't want my family's pride to be tarnished by you getting married to that Omega. He didn't deserve you. He deserved someone much better."

I fisted my hand, doing everything in my power not to punch him in his face so hard that teeth would pop out of his mouth. After all, he was still my father and I still respected him a lot, even though a lot of that respect was gone now.

"You killed your own husband. He was a good person."

A tear broke out and rolled down his cheek.

"Yes, he was, but I didn't want my family to be linked to his family because of you. I didn't even want to remember that you existed." He glanced me over with disdain, wishing he could get rid of me right at this moment.

"Perhaps you should hate me more. I'm going to lock you up in prison myself."

He burst out laughing, regaining his composure moments later. "Based on what? Your word against mine? Do you think the police will trust a biker? If anything, they'll make use of the opportunity to lock you up instead."

I curled up the sides of my lips. I fished my phone out of my pocket and showed it to him.

"Perhaps you should know that I've been recording our conversation this whole time. This should be more than enough to convince the police."

His eyes darted down, lips trembling.

"You fucking asshole," he growled, leaping toward me, but I punched him in his face and stomped on him. I pinned him against the floor, locking my eyes with his.

"You can't stop this anymore. I'm going to have my justice." I pressed my foot more strongly against his chest. I was doing everything in my power not to kill him right now, even though he deserved it. "You should be feeling thankful that Bren convinced me not to kill you."

"Maybe you should do that," he growled when his bodyguards stormed into the room, pointing their guns at me. They were packing silver bullets and they knew that one shot would be enough to immobilize me. More than one shot hitting me and I'd be dead.

The window was open and I jumped through it, landing outside as I raced over to my motorcycle. I plopped down on the seat and fired up the engine, the tires screeching as I raced over to Bren. We chose a meet-up spot so that we could discuss our findings.

I peeked over my shoulders and I couldn't see the bodyguards chasing me, which was concerning. Unless they were planning something I couldn't even begin to guess what it was, they had to be coming after me. I had the recording of my father's confession. I knew that it was going to be enough to put him behind bars.

I pulled over and jumped off the bike as I went into the alleyway. I thought I was going to find Bren in there and already waiting for me, but he was nowhere to be seen. I looked left and right, my heart pounding in my chest.

When I thought I was beginning to hear the rumbling of motorcycles' engines in the distance, my phone started to buzz in the pocket of my pants.

Brent was the only one who had my phone number and I knew that it had to be him. It couldn't be anyone else. Remembering that he was pregnant, I couldn't help but worry about his wellbeing. He needed to pull through and come out of this alive and better than before.

I fished my phone out of my pocket before examining the screen. My hand was trembling when I realized that it was a phone call but that I hadn't picked it up in time.

Shit. Did that mean he tried to call me other times before? I would never forgive myself if he ended up getting hurt because of me. After all, he was only involved in this because of me. I shouldn't have told him about what I knew.

No time to waste, I thought. The Bear Bikers were already coming where I was and I was pretty sure that, this time, they were going to shoot me until they made sure I was dead. They weren't going to make the same mistake twice.

I jumped back on my bike, started the engine, and then rode away to Bren's house. As the wind blew against my face, I had no idea if I was going to have enough time to save him.

All I knew was that I was already getting the police involved in this. Even though I knew that meant probably getting myself locked up too, at least I was going to make sure he was going to be safe.

After all, I had no idea how his Omega father was going to react to him knowing that his son knew about his involvement in the attack.

The tires screeched to a halt as I pulled over, realizing that Ranulf had Bren pinned against the ground in front of his house. He was on top of him, his face showing how much he hated his son.

His bodyguards had me surrounded at a moment's notice, pointing their guns at me. I lifted my hands over my head as I didn't want to do anything that could piss him off.

"Ranulf, I have no idea what he told you, but I already gave the police everything I know, including the recording Bren made of you. They already know about this and they're coming here. Whether you like it or not, you are going to jail, and you'll have a lot to explain about this."

He scoffed, keeping his food pressed against my lover's back.

"The police won't do anything."

After a moment of silence as I realized we weren't going to be making much progress, I said, "I didn't know you hated your son so much. I thought that he meant a lot more to you."

A tear broke out and rolled down his cheek. "I love my son, but I don't want him to end up with you. He deserves someone much better. Everything got so much worse when we realized he was pregnant with your baby."

"I'll do everything in my power to make sure my love is safe."

The skin under his left eye twitched, showing me that he really didn't like that I loved Bren.

He pulled a gun out of his pants, pointing it at me. I felt my eyes changing, becoming more like a wolf's. My canines became bigger as I felt the other side of me coming out.

"I'm not going to let you take my son away from me. I know

the kind of person you are. You will destroy the sweet person he is."

"I would never do anything that could hurt him," I promised, hearing the sound of a bullet coming out of his gun and perforating my chest, my body falling backward over the floor as I realized what was happening.

Ranulf shot me with a silver bullet, and I was going to die.

"Cogwyn!" Bren yelled, leaping toward me. He was right by my side, his hands pushing and nudging me as he tried to make me look at him.

He put his hand on the side of my face, turning my head so that I could look at him. One last look at the face of the man who meant so much to me. The pain in my chest was terrible and was making me think that the bullet most likely hit one of my vital organs. If that was the case, then chances were I wasn't going to pull through.

"You're going to be okay. I promise," Bren murmured when I lost consciousness and didn't know if I was going to wake up again.

BREN'S EPILOGUE

Alright, there was this one thing Cogwyn loved that I just had to bring to him. I opened the door to his room, finding it a little sad that he was still in the hospital bed and that it didn't look like he was going to wake up anytime soon. At least he didn't die... yet, but the police had already said that, if he came out of the coma, they'd lock him up.

I couldn't let that happen. I wasn't going to.

I wasn't worried about that right now, either way. My mind was focused on something else. My ex, Ish, told me that there were a couple of things I could do to remediate the situation. Something that would make Cogwyn remember me and that there were still a couple of things he needed to do, even though he was sleeping.

Sleeping... That's how I liked to think about it. That he was sleeping and that, soon, he'd wake up and realize that I was here, by his side, waiting for him.

My hand was holding a memento from his family. It was a small statue, of a man seated on his motorcycle, doing a wheelie. That was just like him. I remembered that this was in both of his rooms where I had been with him and I was pretty sure that it meant a lot to him.

Outside, I could see the sun shining through the clouds. Winter was ending and I was already looking forward to the coming season.

I pulled a chair, sitting down on it as I opened a book. I was going to read a story to Cogwyn. One other thing Ish said, which I really was happy about, was that me speaking could trigger Cogwyn's brain to wake him up.

Something needed to be done, and I wasn't going to spend my days hoping that he was going to get out of his coma without my help. I was stubborn like that.

I read the first pages of the book after putting down, on the side table, the small statue that I'd found in his belongings. Outside of the room was a police officer. He was just one of the many that were always here in case Cogwyn regained his consciousness.

I didn't pay much attention to him, focusing on the story that I was reading. I thought that my eyes picked up a twitch of his finger, but that couldn't be true. I even stopped reading the words to look up and check his hand, but it was immobile like before and it looked like it was in the same position, too.

I continued reading the story out loud as I noticed, this time, his hand moving and going to his chest. I froze up. This couldn't be happening, right? Cogwyn couldn't be waking up after months of being in a coma.

I was still pregnant and my belly was so much bigger now. If there was a moment for him to wake up, then it was now. Not much longer from now and I'd be delivering the baby...

I dropped the book when I realized that his eyelids were moving up and down, his eyes looking at the ceiling.

"Oh, gosh. My head hurts so much," he mumbled, his hand palming his chest as he pulled one of the cords that were around his body. "What the hell is this?"

I jumped off the chair right away, putting myself right in front of his eyes so that he could see me.

"Bren?" He asked, his voice low and weak. "I knew I could smell you."

"I can't believe you are finally awake!" I exclaimed, smiling from ear to ear.

"That... I'm finally awake?" He asked, narrowing his eyes slightly. "What do you mean? What happened?"

I stepped away from him, not sure how I should approach the subject with him. I didn't want to make him feel more concerned about what happened than he was.

He sat up on the bed, the heart monitoring machine beeping more loudly.

"Tell me everything that happened, Bren. I deserve to know."

"You went into a coma. You've been in a coma here for months since then. I've been waiting this whole time for you to wake up."

He widened his eyes, blinking twice. He looked at his hands as he said, "I'm sorry."

"You don't have anything to be sorry about. It wasn't your fault that things happened this way." Putting my arms out wide, I exclaimed, "But it's really so good to see that you're feeling better. It's like a dream come true."

His eyes darted down, noticing my belly. "I can see that you aren't lying about this, not that I thought you were going to lie about it anyway. Your belly is so much bigger now. I'm going to become a father soon. I suppose I got lucky again."

"You did," I said. "The doctors said that if the bullet had hit you a couple of inches to the right, you'd be dead now."

He curled the side of his lips, chuckling. "I've always been lucky. It's one of the reasons why I ended up falling in love with someone so incredible."

I felt a tear breaking out and rolling down my cheek. "I'm just so fucking happy that you're back."

I ran over to him, hugging him tightly as I buried my head in the crook of his neck. I was sobbing as he put his hand behind my head, drawing small circles on it.

"Shh, don't worry. I'm really back and I'm not going anywhere this time. Once the doctors give me the go-ahead, I'll get out of here and we'll leave the city. I don't think there's any more space for us here."

I was still sobbing when I pulled my head back, looking at his eyes. "Everything will be so much better, but there's something you should know before then."

"What thing?" He asked, lifting his right eyebrow. "You should tell me everything before I get out of this bed."

"It's that the police want to lock you up when you're feeling better," I stammered, wishing that things weren't like this.

He looked over my shoulder, realizing that there was a police officer in front of the door. He had his back turned to us and the wall was thick enough to make it so our conversation wasn't leaking.

Cogwyn pushed the white bedsheet off of his body, groaning as he realized he still felt a lot of pain.

I supported him using the weight of my body, letting him put his arm over my shoulders.

"Be careful. You're a shifter, but you're still human like I am. We need to get out of here before he realizes you're awake."

He regained his balance, now looking like he could stand on his feet without my help. I looked from left to right, wondering what he was scheming.

"What are you planning?" I asked.

"You should draw him into the room and I'll knock him out when he isn't looking."

The plan was very simple, but it should be effective. I went to the door, opened it, and then pointed to the bed as I said hurriedly, "He escaped! I don't know what happened, but when I came into the room, he wasn't in his bed anymore."

"How the hell did he get out?" The police officer asked, drawing out his gun as he started to search the room.

Cogwyn punched the side of his head with his elbow, and the officer's eyes went into his head as he lost consciousness. He fell over on the floor, his gun falling out of his hand.

Cogwyn picked it up and went with me to the hallway. Out in the distance, where the hallways connected, we could see some hospital staff members walking from one room to the other.

"All right, how are we going to do this?" I asked, standing slightly behind him because he was the one who was going to take the lead.

"Just follow me. It's not the first time I've been to this hospital."

I widened my eyes slightly, wondering what story there was in what he said. I didn't have enough time to ask him about that, so I followed him out of the hospital. We had some close calls, but in the end, we soon were in the parking lot.

Cogwyn groaned, looking left and right as he said, "I knew that my bike wasn't here."

COGWYN'S EPILOGUE

Desire wasn't in the hospital's parking lot, but I managed to find it at the police station. It took me some trying and I had to figure out some things about the way things worked there, but I still managed to get my motorcycle back.

We were now living somewhere else, a small house in the woods, where I could hunt, could be happy with my lover, and I could start anew. We were even making new friends, and one of them was an Omega like my lover was.

He was with Bren, holding our baby in his arms. He had such a big and bright smile on his face. I wondered if he was thinking the same thing, that he should also build a family after finding the right person for him.

On my shoulder was a rabbit that I caught when I was hunting in the woods, my feet crunching the snow. Nefion was such a good person I couldn't help but wonder why he was still single and never found someone he wanted to hook up with.

He snapped his head up when he realized I was coming. Cogwyn was just coming out of the house, his hand holding a casserole as he realized that I was already coming back from my hunt.

"Oh, Cogwyn. I didn't realize you were already back. I was just playing with your kid and showing him some new tricks I can do with my hands." And as he finished saying that, he did said tricks, earning some laughs from my baby.

"Well, I'm happy that you two are getting along," I said after putting my rifle down and wrapping my arm over my lover's shoulders. I kissed the side of his face and then his lips, making sure that the kiss wasn't going to last long because I didn't want to make Nefion feel uncomfortable.

I picked up the baby from his arms, loving the fact that he was already moving his small hands toward me, showing me that he recognized I was his father. I rubbed my snot against his face, saying a couple of things over and over that didn't make any sense to me, but which made him chuckle.

The sound of his chuckles was like music to my ears.

Bren handed him the casserole with delicious, homemade food in it, and Nefion picked it up. He lifted the cover and took a peek at it, saying, "Thanks. I'm really going to enjoy this food."

"Please, come back for more. We're trying to fit in."

"I know, it's just that I've got a party that I'm going to throw at my place tonight. I don't suppose you want to come, right?"

"No, we can't," Bren explained, grabbing my hand. "We still haven't managed to find a babysitter for our little one."

"Oh, I could be his babysitter. After all, we get along so well and I always make him laugh."

I looked at Bren, who smiled. "Sure, why not? Wanna start tomorrow?" I asked, remembering that Bren was looking into getting a job and I wanted to be out hunting more often. It looked like the perfect fit, didn't it? Nefion taking care of our little one, Bren fitting in, and me hunting and becoming more like a man of the woods.

Even Desire was beginning to collect some dust in the garage. Don't get me wrong – I still loved riding on my motorcycle, but out here, so far from civilization and hiding from the police in another state, I didn't have another option.

"Then, it's settled. I'll start tomorrow. Should I come here in the morning?"

"Sure, and then maybe you could even start living here with us. Don't worry. We don't have a lot of money, but we'll still pay you fairly for your job. You deserve it."

"Thanks," he said, turning around with the casserole in his hands. "I'm going now, but I'm excited for tomorrow already."

And having said that, he put the casserole on the seat of his car, turned on the engine, and then drove off. We watched until we couldn't see him anymore behind the trees.

We went into the house and I put the baby in his crib, closing the door of his room after cranking up the heater.

I turned, looking at my husband as I lifted his hand and admired the ring on his finger. We got married here, right on this mountain. It was perfect and the snow was always present here. It was always also a little cold, but it wasn't anything that we couldn't handle and we both loved the colder temperatures anyway.

I put my hand on the back of his head, pulling it up for a kiss.

Our lips connected, his body melting in my arms as I had to hold him with my other arm so that he didn't fall.

I pulled my head back, gazing into his eyes as I said, "I love you so much. There's nothing I can do that can express that enough."

"You're wrong. There's one thing," he said, his hand groping my ass and taking off my belt.

"Really? And what would that be?" I asked, feeling my pants dropping as he snuck his fingers under my briefs and looped them around my shaft.

"Making love with me," he answered when I pushed him toward the bed, his body plopping down on it as I climbed on top of him, ripping the clothes off of his body as I started to wet his entrance. Making another baby with my Omega? Sign me up, I thought.

It would be perfect.

OMEGA FOR JEALOUS ALPHA

CHAPTER 1

Nefion

"Yeah, yeah. I'm going there in a bit," I said, looking away from my father. He was in the doorway, glaring at me. It was as though he was doing everything in his power not to kill me. I knew he was hiding something. That look in his eyes didn't fool me, after all.

I pulled up my backpack slightly, going to the bus stop. When I peeked over my shoulder, I couldn't see my father anymore. Thank goodness. Already 19 and I couldn't stop obsessing about this one thing – I needed to move out of my house and find my own place.

Perhaps an apartment in the middle of nowhere. Or in downtown, where I could hit all the gay bars and meet all kinds of different people. Make more friends. I had a lot of them now, but still, more wouldn't hurt.

I couldn't stop thinking of college. That Management degree was going to come in handy when I had it. For one, my uncle said he was going to hire me. My graduation gift and I couldn't wait until I had it. I'd be bossing everyone around, which was something that never happened in my college life.

Just because I was a little shorter than normal, people always assumed that I was supposed to be very submissive. Well, they didn't know anything about me.

I waved my hand over my head when I spotted some of my friends at the bus stop. They were all giggling, chatting, and having a lot of fun. I couldn't wait until we were together and I was having fun with them, too.

The road by my side was packed with cars and motorcycles. I scrunched up my nose at the motorcycles, not liking them one bit. There was just something about bikes that was a turn-off. I smiled gently, thinking that my uncle would be flaying me alive right now if he knew that I thought that way about them.

He thought that everyone loved motorcycles, even though that couldn't be further from the truth. Most of the people that lived in the city thought that way about them, to be honest.

Urgh. I couldn't help but feel like punching them hard for thinking that way. Those motorcycles were polluting the streets, ruining everything, making a lot of noise, and generally making city life pretty unbearable. I just wanted them all gone. Was that something so hard to grasp?

I peeked behind my shoulder when I thought that a certain group of bikers was riding in this direction. Relieved that it wasn't them, I breathed out a sigh of relief. I was thinking that because of a certain rumor floating around. People at college were telling me that my parents were going to pair me with a biker, which couldn't be true.

Right behind the group of my friends at the bus stop was the guy I wanted. He was a couple of years older than I was and hot as balls. Just finding him with my eyes now, I couldn't stop thinking about him and it was pretty obvious that he thought the same way.

Not that I thought anything would ever happen. He hit on me sometimes, especially when we were partying or any time we had the opportunity to talk, but I didn't interact much with him. One of the reasons was that I was focusing on college right now and couldn't be distracted. I just didn't feel ready for a relationship. I didn't feel like having to give someone bucketloads of attention all the time, which was something that was a requirement for that.

I did feel a little bad that I couldn't tell my friends about my first time, though. I thought that I'd eventually find a guy that I was comfortable with, but all the people I knew in college were either rough bros that would certainly hurt me a lot or were too flamboyant. They didn't know this, but I had something for caring, older men, and I couldn't find that at the parties I went to.

I tried hooking up with my crush, but he said he wasn't interested. He said that he was looking for something more permanent, most likely already thinking about the person that he'd marry one day. The thought of getting married didn't cross my mind at all, and thus I couldn't help but feel that it was an alien concept to me. For the time being, anyway.

Although... Fuck. I couldn't stand even remembering that it was going to happen.

There was also the whole thing about fated mates that I couldn't wrap my head around. Who the hell was supposed to confirm that I was going to be someone's fated mate?

It didn't even make sense and, yet, the thing seemed to be trending right now. Apparently, that was happening because of a couple that found out they were always meant to be together and didn't know anything about it until it was too late. They were in an attack in a church somewhere in town.

Pushing that thought out of my mind, I couldn't help but feel that it was nothing more than an illusion. But it was a different kind of illusion, too. I didn't know this for sure, but I was thinking that I knew that couple. They were the ones in the mountain, weren't they?

I didn't know their full story – they kept it locked behind several doors – but they were Alpha and Omega, had a child, and I'd cared for it when I was a couple of years younger.

I couldn't help but hope that the same would happen to my life one day. I didn't think it ever would, though.

Seconds later, when I thought that I was going to be with

my friends and maybe play around with my crush, I felt a strong hand pulling me back. I spun around, meeting the fervent eyes of someone I'd rather not see again.

He was glaring at me and I didn't like the look on his face. He always said that he'd rather see me alone than with someone else.

There was something about him that reeked. He was one of the 'Believers.' One of the people that thought that fated mates existed.

"What are you doing here, Palio?" I grumbled, folding my arms over my chest. As soon as everyone noticed that Palio was with us, they all went silent. I couldn't hear anything other than the cars and the motorcycles driving on the road.

I must've been so focused on spending quality time with my friends that I didn't even notice that he was coming in my direction. Taking a glance over his shoulder, I noticed his motorcycle parked by the sidewalk, the engine turned on. He thought that he wasn't going to have to spend a lot of time here.

"I thought I said I was going to take you to campus myself. I don't like it when you take the bus. It's not safe and you know that it's filled with sex offenders."

I took a look over my shoulder, realizing he was right about that, even if only in part. There were some shady people by the bus stop, but Palio didn't need to worry about them.

He was just being jealous. It wasn't the first time that this was happening. He thought that I was his fated mate and that, one day, we'd get married.

He was a biker. I couldn't help but take mental notes of the black inks on his skin. His tattoos. They defined his being, showed him the kind of person he was, and they made me wonder what his past was like.

He didn't have a lot of money, but he had influence in his motorcycle club. Palio was one of those guys. He felt that he didn't even need to wear a helmet, which was ridiculous and irked me.

I didn't like how he was still keeping me frozen in place with his hand. Not to mention that I could tell the bus was going to come soon and that I'd have to hop onto it. What was this guy thinking he was doing? Was he thinking he was going to throw me onto the seat of his bike and take me to college without my permission?

Things didn't work like that here… Or perhaps they did. I couldn't help but feel submissive in front of him, despite putting up a tough face and glaring back at him.

Palio was a head taller than me and a lot stronger. I didn't doubt that he could wipe the floor with me, though I was sure that was something that would never cross his mind. That he cared a lot about me was evident. I could see it in the way he looked at me, and I could tell that he wasn't going to budge about this, either.

I peeked over my shoulder, realizing that I wasn't going to be able to chat a little with Cynem. My crush was going to have to entertain himself with a girl that kept whoring herself for him, and I couldn't help but feel sorry.

I sighed and sat on Palio's bike. At least I was going to get to college earlier.

CHAPTER 2

Palio

The rumbling of the motorcycle's engine was like music to my ears. Happy that Nefion decided to come along, I twisted the handlebars of the motorcycle and rode off while everyone was staring at us.

They were asking themselves what was happening. If only they knew. I was with my fated mate and even though he always said he didn't want to have anything to do with me, I was pretty sure that his mind would eventually change about it.

He wasn't happy that he had to be hugging me from behind, his body pressed against mine. I was taking him to campus, where I would, unfortunately, have to part ways momentarily with him. I wanted to spend all the time I had with him, and my time was limited, just like everyone else's.

It was no secret that I wanted to spend as much time with him as possible.

I went through hell to find out that he was my fated mate and that we were supposed to marry. I couldn't wait until I was building a family with him, which was one of my dreams.

The wind was blowing against my face and I felt so free I didn't want to get off the bike.

Nefion put his head close to my ear before he said, "You do realize that the whole fated mates thing is ridiculous, right? It's not going to happen. You can't force me to marry you."

I turned my head to look at his eyes, loving how beautiful they were. They were looking right back. Nefion was anything but a coward, which was one of the attributes from him I most liked.

"You might think that way about it at the moment, but your mind will be changed soon. You can be sure of that."

He groaned, pulling his head back. "I'm only doing this because of my father. He has a very strong opinion about us getting married and... I don't want to disappoint him."

I could see where Nefion was coming from. His father was one of the most influential figures in his life and he was such a determined person that it even rubbed off on me. He was an example to be followed, I thought. One day, I was pretty sure that his stressful life would be no more and that he would open a very big smile at our wedding.

His son was mine and was also the most important person in the world for me, which was saying something. So many people marked my life and one day I would thank all of them.

I pulled over, Nefion getting off Destiny and pulling up his backpack. He was looking at me with curious eyes, making me wonder what was going on in his mind right now.

There was this pre-wedding party that we were going to. It was supposed to be a Valentine's Day party and I couldn't wait until I was going there with him. Nefion didn't like it, but I was pretty sure that his mind was going to change about it.

I didn't turn off the engine of the motorcycle. I wasn't coming back here to pick him up and take him home, even though that was something I'd like to do. His dad said that he was going to pick him up and I had to obey all of his wishes, that one included. After all, we were fated mates, but his father's wishes took precedence.

For now, anyway. I couldn't wait until we were living together and I didn't have to tell his parents about what we were doing.

Sniffing his scent, I couldn't help but feel the wolf side of me trying to come out. I wasn't going to let it do that, though. It was locked up inside of me, where it couldn't jump out and ruin my life. I like being a wolf shifter and I had some control over it, but I didn't like it when I wasn't my normal self anymore.

Nefion looked uncomfortable, shifting his weight. It didn't matter how he tried to hide it. The sexual tension between us was very strong and he couldn't conceal it. He couldn't even hide the feelings that he had for me. He knew that I was handsome, tall, and his type.

That was one of the many reasons why we were fated mates.

I approached him, halting when I was right in front of him. Putting my hand on his cheek, I brought his head up as we sealed our lips. We were kissing right in front of the college, where everyone was looking at us and giggling and making snarky comments.

I didn't pay much attention to them, focusing on this exquisite moment. His lips were just so sweet! I could see myself kissing Nefion for hours on end, if only that were possible. Nevertheless, I was very well aware that it wasn't and I was going to keep that in mind.

I didn't use my tongue, even though the kiss was a very passionate one. When I pulled my head back, I could see it in his eyes. He liked it. Nefion didn't want to admit it, but he liked the kiss and craved more.

He was even breathless, which was something that didn't happen often to someone that was on the track team. I took a step backward, still feeling his smell. His scent was something I would always remember. Everyone had a scent and it was always very characteristic and distinctive.

"You shouldn't have kissed me in front of everyone. That wasn't cool."

That was what he was saying, but I knew that it didn't mean

anything. He liked it so much that he was just toying with me. Seeing that, I couldn't help but smile.

"It will never happen again. I promise," I affirmed, getting back on my bike and twisting the handlebars. The engine rumbled to life, making me aware of how powerful my motorcycle was. I could never live without Destiny or the motorcycle club.

He shook his head, spinning around and going to the building where he was going to have his classes. I couldn't wait until we met up again, which I knew was going to happen very soon. Tomorrow, I reminded myself. Tomorrow we were going to meet up again and it was going to be amazing.

Tomorrow was when the Valentine's Day party was going to happen.

Thinking about it, I couldn't help but groan. Even though I wanted to spend as much time with Nefion as possible, there was no denying that the Valentine party was the kind of event I didn't want to spend any time at. It was too well-mannered, too rich, and too extravagant.

But since I couldn't change anything about that, I had to go there.

I stepped onto the pedal, taking off on my motorcycle as I went back to the motorcycle club. Over there, I was going to meet up with the president and pretty much everyone else associated with the club. One of my dreams was to convince Nefion that he should join the club. I knew it would never happen, but maybe one day it could.

I sighed, pulling over when I was by the side of the club. As soon as I was there, I fished out my phone and loaded up a certain app I didn't like using, but which was very much necessary nowadays. If I wanted to stay in touch with Nefion, then I didn't have another choice.

He didn't post anything new on his profile, but I went there anyway to check out his photos. He was just so cute! A little younger than me, but certainly the right person for me.

It wasn't that I was jealous, but there was this guy that also had a crush on him, and I would do anything to fight him off. The problem was that we, the wolf bikers, already had a pretty bad reputation, following recent events between us and the bear bikers.

I heard the door opening and it was the president that was walking out. Striding out, I knew that something was up and that he needed my help with it. The only problem with that was that I didn't want anything major happening in my life right now.

The marriage thing and pretty much everything else that accompanied it was already turning my mind upside down. I had so many things to prepare for and Nefion didn't want to be involved in any of them.

CHAPTER 3

Nefion

It was Valentine's Day and even though I knew I was supposed to be excited about it, I wasn't. I was standing somewhere in the room, holding a glass of water in my hand. Because I wasn't even 21 yet, everyone said that I couldn't drink anything alcoholic, which was bullshit. I couldn't wait until I was a little older so that I could drink anything I wanted.

Meanwhile, all of my friends were busy with other things and with themselves. They were dancing, chatting, and laughing quite loudly, the music reverberating in the room.

This Valentine's Day party was supposed to be a lead-up event before my wedding, but nobody in here cared about me. Not even my parents. They were on the other side of the room, chatting and kissing and generally having a lot of fun, which was something I couldn't have.

And the problem wasn't even with me. I wasn't antisocial or introspective or anything of the sort. I was just like everyone else. But I was realizing that my friends weren't really my friends.

They were always worried about themselves and no one else. When they wanted to hang out with me was when they remembered I existed.

I finished my drink and went over to the bathroom, stumbling on something warm and heavy. I almost lost my balance and fell over on my ass, but a strong hand grabbed my arm and held me in place. Shifting my eyes up, I realized that that person was none other than Cynem, who was regarding me with kind eyes.

His grip wasn't too strong and I could feel the confidence with which he was holding me. Our eyes met and I instantly felt a little confused about my feelings. There was no denying that he was hot, but was that really the only thing I felt for him?

I didn't know, but he was my only shot at turning the tables. I wanted to make this party better than it was, even though that was going to be very difficult. When they chose the music for the party, they didn't think it through.

They chose some of the worst music.

He let go of my arm before rubbing the back of his head. "Sorry about that. I meant to warn you before, but I didn't have enough time."

Now that he was filling my vision, I couldn't help but feel I had even forgotten about Palio. He was supposed to be somewhere at the party, but I couldn't see him. Maybe he finally realized that I didn't want to have anything to do with him...

It didn't matter how much he tried to make me understand I was his fated mate, I would never believe him. That was a promise I was making to myself.

And it wasn't like I could smell his scent at the party. It was strong and certainly very distinctive, but there were far too many people in the room. I couldn't even smell the scent of the guy that was in front of me and that was saying something, considering how intense it was.

I tried to smile, saying, "It's okay. I know it wasn't your fault."

He kept looking at me for what felt like an eternity, making me wonder what was going on in his mind. When I opened and closed my mouth, he said, "Do you wanna go outside with me? I don't mean to insult, but this party is trash. You deserve something better, like this bottle of wine."

As soon as he finished saying that, he produced a bottle of wine, lifting it in his hand. I didn't know anything about wines, but the bottle looked pretty cool. A touch on it and I could tell that it was pretty cold, too. Licking my lips, I couldn't help but feel like going outside with him to empty it.

I checked around us, noticing that no one was looking at us. It was one of the benefits of people not giving a damn about me, I thought. It didn't even make sense. They came to this party because of me. There was even a huge neon sign hanging from one of the walls, mentioning my name and Palio's.

I didn't know what was going on in their minds, but I had enough of them and this party. Thinking that, the first thing that popped up in my mind was, "I don't want to spend a second longer here."

He widened his smile, turning around when I felt a scent in the air, and I couldn't overlook it. The first thought that came into my mind was that this couldn't be happening. The first time that I was finally letting loose and was ready to take the first step with Cynem, HE was going to show up.

I turned around again, finding Palio standing right behind me. He looked different, unlike his normal biker self. He had a suit on with a red tie, something that I thought not even in a million years would happen. He was even holding a single red rose in his hand, which was also just as mind-boggling. Him being the tough biker he was, I couldn't believe he ever would look more… refined.

He even got a haircut and did his beard before coming. Palio still stood out, but nobody could say that he wasn't giving his all.

His eyes were trembling slightly, showing me that something terrible was happening, and I didn't want to think about it. I wanted to pretend that this wasn't happening. It couldn't end well at all.

I could see his eyes changing, becoming more wolflike.

I tried to stand between the two of them, but Cynem pushed me aside. He didn't do it to hurt me, but because he had a score to settle with Palio. The two were about the same height and stature, making me wonder who would win in a fight. Palio was older and more experienced, which should give him an edge.

"You shouldn't be here," Palio growled, stepping toward his nemesis.

"Why not? You left your fiancé unattended and I was going to keep him company, something that you are obviously not fit for."

"You don't know anything about me," Palio argued, shoving Cynem gently. He wasn't trying to start a fight. He only shoved Cynem because he wanted to make his point clear. Either Cynem left us or something bad would happen.

"I know a lot about you. I know you are a wolf biker and that you shouldn't even be trying to marry someone so much younger than you. You got it in your head that you are his fated mate, which couldn't be any further from the truth. I don't believe in that sort of bullshit, which is why I'm telling you this – leave him alone before I make you regret it."

Blood was rushing to my head, making me feel tenser. This didn't look good at all. Everyone around us was still dancing and chatting, not even realizing the weight of what was happening. They were both alphas. They were so strong that a fight in here would destroy the party and it would mar my wedding, which wasn't something I wanted. I didn't want the wedding to happen, but not this way.

I stepped to stand between the two of them, turning my head from side to side.

"Hey, the two of you. Stop fighting. I don't like it when you fight."

Cynem looked down, finding my eyes. I thought he was going to object, but then he said, "Fine, but I'm only doing this for you. You don't want a fight to break out at the party and it won't. I promise you that."

After saying that, he turned around and left, leaving me wondering what was going on in his head. Did he still have such a strong crush on me? I didn't know, but everything was pointing toward that being the case, which was puzzling.

I was confused about my feelings toward him, which couldn't be good. After all, I was going to get married to someone else, who was less than pleased about having competition.

I turned again, looking right into Palio's eyes. He was shifting back to his normal self. His eyes went back to normal, which was very relieving.

"Why the hell did you say those things to him?" I asked, putting my hands on my waist. "He's a good person. He knows the limits and that he can't have me. I don't like you much, but since my father is forcing me to marry you, I'll have to."

He shook his head, saying, "You don't understand anything."

And as he finished saying that, I couldn't help but wonder why he did. What was it about us that I didn't understand?

CHAPTER 4

Palio

Cynem couldn't touch a follicle of his hair and I wasn't going to allow him. I would never. Nefion was mine. He was going to be my husband soon and I couldn't wait until I was putting the marriage ring on his finger, kissing his lips in front of everyone in the church.

I put my hand on his shoulder, leading him out of the party. He peeked over his shoulder, saying, "Hey, where the hell do you think you're taking me?"

"Out of here, for starters. Nothing good will come out of this party. Not to mention that I don't feel comfortable here anyway."

I thought he was going to object, but he was coming along as everyone kept ignoring us. As usual, they came to this party for themselves and no one else. I needed to keep that in mind.

"At least that's something we can agree on," he joked, opening the exit door and stepping out with me. We were in an alleyway between two buildings, happy that the pounding music wasn't shattering our eardrums anymore.

"Gosh, I feel like I can finally breathe again," he added, turning around and giving me the right opportunity to give him something else that I had with me. It was in the pocket of my pants. It was pretty small and was supposed to accompany the rose I had in my other hand.

I fished it out, moving my arm around him and showing him the rose first. He didn't mind that I was behind him and touching him, which was perfect. One of the reasons I was doing this was a pretty simple one. I needed to win his heart over.

I was pretty sure that doing that was going to be easy. After all, he was my fated mate, but I still needed to put the effort in. That's what this was all about. Not to mention that I loved him now that I knew he was my fated mate.

Nefion looked down, finding the rose in my hand. He picked it up slowly, saying, "It looks beautiful. I never thought that a biker like you actually had an eye for this kind of thing."

"Still thinking that I'm only a brute and don't know how to show niceness sometimes?" I asked, not feeling insulted by that. I knew the reputation that preceded wolf bikers like me. Everyone thought that we were just criminals. It wasn't like that at all. We were different, tougher, a little more ruthless than normal, but we were still people like everyone else.

"Something like that," he said, chuckling gently. "You got it just for me?"

"Yup," I responded, leaning in and smelling his scent through his perfume. It didn't matter how much perfume he sprayed on himself, his scent was always going to be strong and I was always going to know what it was like. There was no denying that.

I could already imagine our lives being like this for years on end, which was something I was looking forward to.

I moved my other arm so that my hand was showing him the other gift I bought. It was an engraved necklace, which made his eyes sparkle as soon as he noticed them. For a moment, he didn't know what to say.

"I also got this for you. It's supposed to make you remember me, wherever you are."

This was all happening because even though Nefion always pretended that he hated me, I knew he thought differently. I knew that he liked me, deep down there in his heart. It was just going to take him a while until he let that part of him out.

I shifted so that I was putting the necklace around his neck, and then I moved closer, pressing my body against his again. I was finding it very hard not to have an erection right now, which I was pretty sure he appreciated. He was the kind of guy that didn't like it when someone was being forceful to him.

And I wasn't going to be. I wanted to win his heart over and not force him to like me. Or at least, to force him to show me the true feelings he felt about us.

"It's really beautiful. It's even more beautiful than the rose, which is something I didn't think possible."

At this moment, I had already forgotten about Cynem and his attempts to steal my lover's heart. I thought that Nefion had already made it pretty clear that he wasn't interested.

I pondered kissing his cheek, but decided not to. Even though we kissed that time in front of his college, things were different now. I wanted him to take the other steps to building our relationship. I wanted him to be more proactive.

I moved away from him, happy when he said, "You've impressed me more than I thought you ever could."

"What can I say?" I said, smiling broadly. "I'm always like that. I'm always obsessed with you, and I just want to see you happy."

He took some steps toward me, putting his hands on my waist. His eyes were locked with me and what I did next felt natural. I put my hands on his jaws, pulled his head up, and then sealed our lips again. It was just like that time. His lips were very sweet and our kiss was extremely passionate.

There was no denying that he was falling more and more in love with me.

The kiss was so good that I closed my eyes and didn't think of anything in particular, just focusing on how much I wanted it to mean a lot more than it did.

He pulled his head back, regarding me with passionate eyes.

"I don't like you much, but if there's something you are good at, it's kissing," he purred, still not moving his hands away. I thought he was going to. It would be just like him to do something like that when it looked like things were going in my favor.

I put my arm around his shoulders and then started walking with him toward the parking space by the building. I didn't even worry that someone would come out looking for us. They most likely weren't going to.

"Where are you taking me this time?" He quizzed, not trying to move away from me. He was indeed coming with me. Nefion was curious and wanted to find out what I was thinking.

We rounded the corner of the building, finding the parking space and my motorcycle. Destiny was parked on one of the spots, just idling there. It looked pretty beautiful, especially under the gentle moonlight.

"I'm going to take you to a breathtaking spot. You deserve something a lot better than this shitty party."

He craned his head to look at me, saying, "I like the sound of that."

I sat on my motorcycle, put him on the backseat, and then revved up the engine. We took off moments later, the wind blowing against our faces. We didn't even look back to see if any of the partygoers had come out searching for us. They hadn't.

I took him through the streets and neighborhoods, stopping when we reached a hill. It overlooked the city and was the perfect spot for this special day that preceded our marriage.

I parked the motorcycle and he got off of it, stepping toward the edge of the hill. He was overlooking the city, eyes sparkling. I approached him from behind before I said, "You've never been here, have you?"

He shook his head gently.

"It's so beautiful. I didn't think a place like this existed."

"There's a lot about the city you don't know. Thankfully, now you finally have someone who can teach you everything about it."

I wrapped my arms around his lower torso, bringing him closer to me. He didn't object, and I knew, from the start, he wasn't going to. I could feel his scent, his perfume, and the warmth of his body.

I could just imagine taking him to my bed, which I imagined he was also thinking about right now. But I wasn't going to. This was Valentine's Day, but we weren't boyfriends. It was a pity that we weren't, but there was nothing I could do about it.

"Maybe you aren't so bad after all," he purred, kissing me again and making me happy that we were. I could just imagine what our wedding was going to look like. I could imagine all the flowers that were going to decorate the church, the people inside it, the song that was going to play when he was coming toward me, and pretty much everything else my mind could conjure at the moment.

I wanted to make all of that happen and I couldn't wait until it was.

CHAPTER 5

Nefion

My heart was tight, but after everything he showed me, I thought that I could make this work. I was getting wedded, but it didn't mean that I was going to have to live with Palio for the rest of my life, right? I was going to get to know him better, which I knew was supposed to happen before the wedding, but here I was.

I shook my head at the thought, feeling my father's arm around mine. We were outside the church, just waiting for the right moment to step in. Someone inside the church was going to signal for us to walk in, and I was anxious about that.

I could see my future husband waiting for me on the other end of the room, with his hands crossed over his crotch. He was looking so professional and unlike his normal self, which was interesting.

He could be anyone he wanted, but he decided to become a biker. That was one question I needed to ask him when we were living alone in his house.

He wasn't rich, but he managed to finance his house. It wasn't very big. It didn't have everything I wanted, but it was better than nothing. Certainly a lot better than living in my parents' house, which was already very relieving. Just thinking that I wasn't going to have to go there after the wedding was already bringing a smile to my face.

I turned my head to look at my father, who was staring ahead with focused eyes. I had no idea what was going on in his mind and I wanted to probe it.

"Dad, do you really believe in all that fated mates bullshit?" I asked, knowing that I was probably crossing a line. It was better asking now when I still had time for that, I concluded. After the wedding, I didn't know when we would see each other again.

He turned his head to look at me, narrowing his eyes slightly.

"What kind of question is that? Do you even know what Palio went through to find out if we were right?"

I bit my bottom lip, realizing that, this whole time, I never bothered to ask them about it. I was so focused on college and graduating that I didn't even remember to do something as simple as that.

"That you were right?" I asked, feeling a little confused about that. I thought that he said they were going to find out who his partner was. "Do you mean that you already knew I was supposed to be his fated mate?"

It took him a while to respond, which was only making this more confusing to me. I didn't want to think that it was a red flag, but it looked like it was. I was a little terrified, but I wasn't going to back off on the wedding. I was going to go through with it.

After all, we already spent so much money and effort on making sure that everything was going to be right. Even my outfit was one of the most expensive things I had ever seen in my life.

"We suspected you might be. We were going to confirm it using the Sphere of Revelations, but you know what happened to it. It was shattered during an attack. I hate those Bear Bikers so much I want to see all of them dead. One day, they will pay for everything they did."

He was spitting saliva out of his mouth, making me feel the

rage that was bubbling in his veins. If it was up to him, he would do a lot worse than that. I had never seen my father so angry before.

He was my Alpha father. My Omega father was inside the church, seated on one of the front benches. He was looking over his shoulder at us and wondering when we were going to be allowed in.

I turned my head to look back inside the room, just waiting for the song to kick in. When I breathed in and thought that it was still going to take a while until that happened, that's when it did.

I saw someone inside the church signaling for us to walk in, which we did. We crossed the front entrance and were soon walking down the aisle, everyone standing up and clapping.

It didn't matter how much I thought everything was wrong about the wedding. Now that it was finally happening and everything inside the main chamber looked so bright and beautiful, I couldn't imagine myself doing anything different.

I checked pretty much everyone that was in the chamber, clapping so loudly I couldn't hear anything else. Everyone that I knew from college was here, which was very exciting.

I could already see it happening. I could already imagine them talking about the wedding online for days on end. We lived in a medium-sized city, which meant that the marriage was a very important event, but wasn't the most striking one.

My father halted with me when we were in front of my husband. He took his arm off of me and then shook my future husband's hand, opening a big, bright smile. Unlike so many people in the city, he had no problem marrying me to a biker. He was actually okay with it.

After they shook their hands, my father went to one of the benches. It was where my Omega father was seated. When he was seated by his side, they held her hands together and waited for the continuation of the wedding.

I turned slowly, finding my future husband's eyes. They were full of love for me and how much he wanted me to be happy. It was great that he was feeling that way about it, but I couldn't shake off the feeling that something tiny was wrong about this. It was almost imperceptible, but I couldn't stop thinking about it.

And it was pointless to try and figure out what it was. I didn't think I could do that.

I sighed, trying to feel a tiny little happier about this than I was, just so that I could shake that feeling off and focus on the good aspects of getting wedded. It meant that I was going to live a different life and cease feeling like a teenager, which wasn't good.

I took a glance around the chamber, not finding someone that popped up in my mind all of a sudden. Palio could never know that the thought was in my mind right now. Cynem and his charming presence. I was pretty sure that news of the wedding was affecting him greatly and I couldn't do anything about that.

I knew that he liked me, but I thought that he'd already have shaken it off and focused on better things. After all, he'd already dated many Omegas. Was I really someone so dear to him? I didn't know but, either way, I'd like to make it so I wasn't saddening him.

I sighed, the priest reciting words from a book. A sudden thought popped up in my mind. I thought that bikers were supposed to marry their loved ones on the road. I'd seen documentaries about it. Bikers usually got wedded while riding on their motorcycles and not in churches.

Palio was different from his kin, and I couldn't help but wonder why. I supposed that he was doing this to please my father, who didn't have anything to do with any motorcycle club.

His MC buddies weren't here either, which only sprouted more questions in my mind. I didn't know what was going on, but it was difficult to focus on anything else when my future husband was already putting the marriage ring on my finger.

Then, I did the same for him. He cupped my face with his firm hands and we kissed, everyone clapping after the priest said we were husband… and husband. I chuckled at the thought, at the moment focusing on just one thing – how sweet and needy his kiss was.

It was like he was releasing everything he'd been obsessing over this whole time. He was kissing me with delight, only pulling his head back when he had his fill.

I was breathless, my lungs expanding and contracting. There was something different about that kiss I couldn't put my finger on. Even though I couldn't tell what he was thinking about right now, I could say that our wedding night was going to happen one way or another. And Palio being a biker, I couldn't help but wonder if he was going to do something different from what most people normally would.

"Time to go, love," he said, taking my hand and leading me down the aisle again. We stepped out of the church and everyone gathered around us, throwing rice over our heads. We ducked and climbed up his motorcycle. Nobody was going to follow us, which was something I was happy about.

We finally had privacy and the world was ours to tackle.

CHAPTER 6

Palio

I was happy beyond anything I had ever felt before, standing behind the door to our room. I got a house just for us, which I knew he was happy about. I wrapped my fingers around the doorknob and then twisted it, opening the door.

Our room was very simple, but it was enough. Nefion was already taking off his clothes. He looked so pretty and inviting. He had his earbuds on, which meant he couldn't hear that I was walking in.

I closed the door gently behind me, stepping toward him before wrapping my arms around his torso. I kissed the nape of his neck and then took off his earbuds, loving the way his warmth was pulsing out of his body.

"You look so lovely, dear," I murmured, peppering the side of his neck again and again. We were fated mates and there was no doubt about that. When I was by his side, I couldn't think about anything else. All I could think about was how much I loved him and how much I wanted to spend as much time with him as possible.

"You caught me off guard."

"Does that bother you?" I asked, helping him unbutton his shirt. I was finally feeling it. His bare, exposed skin, and it was different from everything I had felt before. It was so warm and smooth, unlike my body. He was going to feel it too when I took off my clothes, I thought, purring against his neck.

"Not at all," he replied, taking off his shirt and melting in my arms. I moved my hands over his shoulders, massaging him. I loved how smooth and soft his skin was, and I couldn't help but pepper it with several more kisses.

He squirmed, grinding his body against me as his ass rubbed against my crotch. Gosh, he was turning me on so much I was already getting an erection. I was already thinking about throwing his legs open and burying my cock inside of him, which I was very sure he wanted as well.

I brushed my finger over his lips, turning him around slowly before I sealed my lips to his again. He melted in my arms again, held in place by them. If it wasn't for them, he would be falling on the floor.

I dug my tongue into his mouth, battling against his tongue for what felt like an eternity. Nefion was an Omega who wanted me to knock him up, but he was also braver than most other Omegas. He could stand up for himself, which was very unlike his kind.

His lips brushing against me, I couldn't help but push him against the wall, though I did so gently. I didn't want to hurt him and I never would. Not to mention that I would never forgive myself if something like that happened.

My dick was just so hard and I couldn't wait until I was knotting him. I was pretty sure that the same thought was swirling around in his mind, too.

Moments later, I pulled my head back and I noticed that he was breathless. He was trying to breathe, but he was having difficulty doing so. I let a couple of moments pass and when I noticed that he was already feeling better, I got on my knees and started to unbuckle his belt.

I looked up, noticing that his lips were parted. He nodded and I went ahead, happy that I got my confirmation. I took off his belt and his pants fell to the floor, finally revealing my prize. I loved how big his bulge was and that his cock was already hard. I could even see a stain of pre-come on the fabric.

No denying it. I was going to knot him on our wedding night, already building toward having one of the best families in the world. Even though it was going to be difficult and a little weird, it was also going to be great.

I'd also have to come clear to the president and tell him that I wasn't going to be a part of the club anymore, but that was okay. I was pretty sure he was going to understand it.

His scent was stronger now than it had ever been, impregnating my lungs. I basked myself in it and then started to lower his pair of briefs, which made him a little uncomfortable. I thought he was going to ask me to stop and take things a little slower, but he didn't.

He was going to lose his virginity and there was nothing he could do to stop it. I mean, there was, but he was already too invested in it to ask me to stop now.

I finished pulling his pair of briefs down, loving the way his cock came jumping out. It was bouncing up and down, pre-come seeping out of the slit. I grabbed it and lowered my head, sticking my tongue out. I brushed it over the tip of his cockhead, finally getting a taste of his release.

He groaned, closing his eyes. With the help of my other hand, I took him to the bed, where he sat. He was in the perfect position for what I was looking for to do with him. I gave his cock a couple of strokes, making sure that I was giving him as much pleasure as possible.

My heart was pounding in my chest, which was something that didn't happen often, even when I was having sex with another guy.

I looked up, noticing that his eyes were still closed. Opening a dirty smile, I dove down and wrapped my lips around his shaft. I worked first on the cockhead, loving the shape of it. His body was trembling, pleasure all over it.

Nefion was feeling so much lust I was already wondering what he was going to feel like when I was inside of him. Moments later, I lowered my head as I put more of his shaft inside my mouth.

Playing with his balls, I thought he was going to come when his dick started to spasm between my lips, but it was just a false flag.

"Knot me," he purred, making me widen my smile. There was nothing better than hearing that coming from my love.

"With pleasure," I said, getting off his cock and laying him down on the bed. I turned him around, took off my clothes, and started to stroke my cock. My shaft was already hard. Nefion was so wet right now I knew I could breach him without lube. Thinking that, I smiled again as I climbed up the bed and grabbed him by his waist.

He gripped the bedsheets tightly when I nudged his orifice with my cock. I was just playing with him in the beginning, wondering how he was feeling about this. His body was covered in sweat, and it looked like he was ready. And as long as he was ready, so was I.

I stayed still for a couple of moments, wondering what was going on in his mind right now.

I pushed myself into his orifice as I breached it, going all the way to the bottom. Rolling my hips, I started to pound in and out of him, loving the way we were becoming one. My dick grew bigger than it had ever been and I knew that now I'd only get out of him after I knotted him. He was moaning and groaning, pleasure spreading all over his body.

I increased my pace when I felt more comfortable inside of him. I kicked it up a notch when I was even more comfortable with how things were happening. He started to match me thrust for thrust, which made our sex even better.

Nefion felt so small underneath me and if there was one

other thing I was thinking about right now, it was how much I needed to protect him from everything and anyone that wanted to harm him.

And then I came inside of him, knowing that I was knocking him up and that there was no turning back. Now that I was inside of him, I knew he was going to have my baby. I wasn't going to stop with just one baby, though.

When my dick stopped throbbing inside of him, I pulled out and fell down onto the bed. Wrapping my arms around him, I snuggled him between them and we fell asleep.

I couldn't wait until I found out what the days ahead had in store for us.

CHAPTER 7

Nefion

What happened that night was amazing and I'd never forget it. After a hot shower, Palio was already opening the door of the bathroom and wrapping his arms around me. He caught me off guard again, which was something that wasn't supposed to happen.

I didn't know what was up with my nose, but I should have noticed him coming, especially now that my mind was used to the fact that he was my husband.

The badass biker was my husband. We were living in a very small house, but it all still felt so odd. He shouldn't be looking to settle down with anyone. Looking up and at his eyes, though, I couldn't help but realize that his love for me was genuine. I just kind of wished he wasn't so obsessed with me all the time. I was pretty sure that one of these days I'd snap, shouting at his face that he wasn't supposed to catch me off guard so often.

Right now, though, it was the day after the wedding and I couldn't think of those things. I just let his firm arms melt me in them, his lips going for the nape of my neck and pecking it. I melted in his embrace once more and could see the same happening in all the days that were going to follow this one.

Even though I was married, I wasn't sure about the whole 'fated mates' thing. I supposed I needed to get to know him better before even considering anything along the lines of a divorce, though.

"You look so lovely this morning," he purred, looking at my reflection in the mirror. He was naked, as was I. His dick was already hard, making me think that he was planning on knotting me again soon. While I wanted that, I was pretty sure that he had his own things to take care of.

Not to mention that I was planning on going to the library for studies. There were so many things I needed to read and assimilate. My degree was a very difficult one and I was pretty sure he was well aware of that.

I pecked his lips, saying, "And you look just as lovely. I didn't think that getting married was going to change my life so much."

"It's only the beginning," he said, moving his hand over my belly and making me remember that something ground-breaking happened the other night. I was so worried about some other things that the thought didn't cross my mind until it was already too late. He really knotted me. I mean, I guess that the thought must have popped up sometime in my mind, but I must have brushed it off. I didn't think that this biker was so in love with me that he wanted me to have his baby.

My breathing quickened. It was one thing not thinking something and another letting something like that happen. I should've been more cautious, even though I supposed that, now, it was too late and I couldn't do anything about it. Short of getting an abortion, which I didn't think I could, there was no viable alternative. I didn't want to feel that I was killing a life. That was a thought that always popped up in my mind when the word 'abortion' was brought up.

"Something wrong?" He asked, stopping the movement of his hand around my belly.

"No. Don't worry about it. I was just concerned with my midterm - the one that I'll have tomorrow morning. I need to be ready for it. You know how important getting my degree is."

He softened his expression now that he realized it wasn't anything he should be worried about. He moved his hand down, grabbing my balls and giving them a little squeeze. I closed my eyes, letting waves of pleasure move through my body. It was difficult to think that anything was wrong with our life when he was already making me feel this way.

He pulled his hand back, keeping his body pushing against me. He was just hugging me from behind, feeling the warmth of my body.

But the thing about growing a life inside my belly was true. I didn't know if I wanted it or even if I was ready for it. Not to mention that I didn't think I would have time to care for a baby.

Moments later, Palio stepped away from me and went back into the room, where he put on his clothes. After he finished adjusting his leather jacket with the insignia of his motorcycle club, he said, "I need to go see the president. He's waiting for me."

Looking at him through the reflection in the mirror as I did my hair, I asked, "To do what?"

"I can't be your husband, the father of our little one, and a biker at the same time. I know it's a difficult decision and I pondered once about convincing you to join the club, but I couldn't. My mind is made up."

I blinked twice, finding that surprising. Never thought that Palio would consider inviting me into the club. Now that he mentioned that, I was thinking that it would be pretty cool, though only for a day.

I would do it just to see what being a biker was like from their point of view. It wasn't like I would suddenly decide that becoming a biker was what I wanted. After all, there was nothing worse than contradicting myself. I had always hated bikers and that would never change, even though Palio was changing a lot about the way I looked at them.

He came to me and gave me one last kiss, saying, "I'll be back soon. It should take me only a couple of hours to go through the process. I'm pretty sure that the president will think I'm betraying him. After all, he likes me a lot. It will be fine, though. He'll realize that he can't keep me there forever."

I checked his expression, realizing that he was speaking the truth.

I put the comb down on the sink before saying, "If you say so, but if anything happens, don't hesitate to call my father. He'd be happy to help you. Not to mention that he's probably looking for a bodyguard. You could work for him."

He smiled without showing his teeth, and even though he was trying to show that he was comfortable about this, I could tell that he wasn't. I didn't know what was about it, but it looked like he wasn't keen on the idea of working for my father.

He kissed me again before going out and climbed up on his bike, riding away. I was outside the house, looking at him as he went and turned left. When he was out of sight, I turned back around before noticing that someone was coming in my direction.

The first thought that popped up in my mind was that it was a criminal trying to rob me, but after turning again and checking out who it was, I was surprised when I realized it was none other than Cynem.

I didn't think he was going to show up all of a sudden. The fact that he did rang some alarms in my mind. What if he had been waiting outside until I wasn't with my husband anymore?

I didn't know, but I was still cautious.

His feet halted in front of me as he opened a smile. "Nefion, I'm so sorry about it. I meant to come to the wedding, but I couldn't. I was caught up in something."

I blinked twice, happy that he was mentioning the wedding and the fact that he hadn't been in it.

"It's okay. You're here now and that's what matters."

That's what I said, but I still wanted to punch his face so hard that he wasn't at the wedding. I didn't know what was about it, but I wanted his approval as well. I wanted things to be okay between us, and I was pretty sure that he thought the same way. After all, even though we had once tried to be lovers, it didn't have to mean we couldn't be friends.

A moment of silence ensued and I wondered what he was thinking about. He looked up, finding my eyes and when I was going to open my mouth to invite him in, he grabbed my face and kissed me.

I pushed him away from me, stumbling back into my house. I narrowed my eyes as I blushed.

"What was that?" I barked, not liking that he was leering at me.

He approached me, looking very much determined about what he was doing.

"I came here for you. I miss you so much, and there's something about Palio you need to know."

CHAPTER 8

Nefion

I shook my head, stepping farther into my house as I tried to shut the door. But he put his hand against it, preventing me from doing that. Seconds later, he was stepping into my house as well, and then he closed the door behind him. I had no idea what was going on in his mind, but I wasn't interested.

My hand went for my phone, I fished it out of my pocket, and when I tried to call the police, he snatched it from me and put it on a side table. He was trying to show me that he came here in peace, but I knew better. As far as I was concerned, he invaded my house and needed to be kicked out of it as soon as possible.

"Cynem, you're going to regret this," I warned, going to the kitchen and grabbing a knife. Pointing it against him, I did everything in my power to show him that I wasn't kidding. If he tried anything similar to what he did, I wouldn't be opposed to hurting him.

He stepped toward me, grabbed my wrist, and lowered it as I realized I didn't have enough strength to fight him. Not to mention that he was an Alpha, much stronger than me, and also a wolf shifter.

I could see it in his eyes, the way that they were changing and becoming more wolflike. His fur was beginning to show as well, which wasn't good news. I didn't want him to transform. Unlike

Palio, he couldn't control that other side of him.

I put the knife back down by the side of the sink as he locked his eyes with me again.

"I know I lost you, but maybe not all hope is lost."

And after a moment of silence, he asked, "He knocked you up, didn't he?"

I waited to see if he was going to do anything else. When I realized that he wasn't going to back off, I responded, "I don't think that's something you need to know anything about. It's none of your business."

He shook his head. "I'm just trying to help you. How much do you think you know about Palio?"

"That he's a much better person than you."

"If that's the way you think of it, then I'm disappointed in you. You used to be much more of a fighter."

I tipped up my chin. Even though he was an Alpha and I was just an Omega, he wasn't going to change my mind about the wedding. I was looking forward to the life I was going to have with my husband, which was a lot more than anything else I ever had in my life.

"I'm still the same person. It's you who changed. You'd never have kissed me the way you did."

"You don't know anything about me," he affirmed, growling and grabbing my face with his hand, digging his fingers into my skin. I felt powerless. It was his power over me that was making me do nothing. I tried to fight against him, but it was impossible.

"You are hurting me."

As soon as I said that, he pulled his hand back and stepped away from me. I fell on my knees on the floor, panting. I never thought that the guy who was my crush would do what he did. He was ruthless, his body changing still.

"I know that Palio is ditching the gang. I'll join them and replace him."

I looked up, finding him with his back turned to me. I could see tears forming in his shirt and pants, signaling his ongoing transformation. I had no idea what was going on in his mind, but it was scaring me. I didn't have my phone with me. I wanted to call the police before he hurt me again.

"What?" I asked, finding his affirmation hard to grasp. "I know he's going to do that, but what do you have to do with it? It has no relation to you."

He turned around slowly, his eyes holding me as though he was pondering if he should eat me alive. I was so scared that my skin was cold. My heart was so tight I thought I was going to have a heart attack.

"I'm going to replace him. I'm going to take his place, become the next sergeant at arms, and then I'll kill him. I can never forgive him for what he did."

I stood up slowly, supporting my weight against the wall.

"And what did he do against you?"

"There's something you need to know. You remember that I came from the Land of Nanape, don't you?" Just as he finished saying that, he stepped toward me and when I thought he was going to hit me, his expression softened up.

I remembered what happened in Nanape. The kind of things that happened there, the war, and the number of people who died in their land... I could never forget that. It had been all over the news. I usually was the kind of person who tried to understand other people's points of view, so it wasn't surprising that the war shook me to the core.

"I can never forget what happened in Nanape, but what does it have to do with anything we are discussing?" I asked, feeling breathless.

"It feels as though everything was staged, but it wasn't. You didn't know that Palio was in the war, fighting for our country. You don't know the kind of things he did. There's a reason why he is a Wolf Biker. He killed so many people, my parents included. I found out about it not too long ago. You don't know how long I've been looking for the truth."

I blinked slowly, stepping away from him. Putting as much distance as possible between us was necessary right now. He was huge, very imposing, and his presence alone was enough to make anyone turn their attention to him.

"I think you got it wrong. Palio was never in the war and he never killed anyone. He is not a criminal or a sadist."

He scoffed, pulling out his phone. He turned it so that I could see what the screen was showing me, smirking when he realized I understood he was right.

The video was showing everything, which was confusing and enlightening at the same time. Palio had indeed been in the war, unless this was some kind of well-made deep fake video. Knowing how well technology was advancing, that could be the case, but something in my heart was telling me it wasn't.

I now had several questions to ask Palio and I didn't know if I had the courage to do that.

"And how do you know he really was involved when your parents were killed?"

"I can't tell you that. I can't show you the document, but it says specifically that he was involved. He was part of the mission where they killed everyone in my city."

Studying his face, I could tell he wasn't lying about any of what he was saying. Nevertheless, whether he was truly saying the truth or not didn't matter. What mattered was that he was raging. He was so much more than angry. He wanted to rip open Palio's neck and that was putting it mildly.

I didn't think I'd ever seen someone so angry before.

"I can't let you do that. You used to be a better person than this," I lamented, walking past him and wondering if he was going to stop me. I picked up my phone as I studied what he was going to do. I thought he was going to lunge at me, but he held his ground for a couple of seconds. When he realized that I wasn't going to change my mind, he walked out of the house.

He halted, turning around to peek over his shoulder. He was looking at me when he said, "You should ditch him, too. He lied to you about his past, didn't he?"

I opened my mouth, but there was nothing that could be said. I knew he was right, even though it was just in part. Palio never lied about his past, but I also never asked him about it.

Satisfied with my lack of answer, Cynem turned left and started to walk away. When he was out of sight, I already felt much more relieved. I walked back into the house, sat on the floor, and started crying against my knees.

I couldn't believe that everything appeared to be spiraling out of control. I couldn't believe that someone already had it in for my husband, who was someone I was beginning to like.

I had no idea what was going to happen, but when he was back home, I needed to confront him about it.

CHAPTER 9

Palio

The president slammed his hand against the table, looking across it at me. "You have no right to be doing this. You're the most important citizen of the pack."

"I'm sorry, but it has to be done. I'm married now," I said, lifting my hand and showing him the marriage ring. He glanced at it, remembering that he'd been in the wedding and couldn't have done anything to stop it, even though he wanted to do so quite a lot.

"This is a mistake. You know that the Bear Bikers have it in for us. We need you to keep them at bay."

"I'm aware of that, but you'll be fine." I rounded the table, putting myself in front of him. After putting my hand on his shoulder, I affirmed, "Even without me, you'll be fine. I'm sure of it."

He ran his hand through his thick, bushy beard, sighing and stepping away from me. He was looking at the window when someone knocked on the door. "Boss, you have a visitor and he wants to talk to you."

The president turned around, looking at me with quizzing eyes. I shrugged and he shuffled over to the door, opening it. While the Wolf Bikers were a large group, he didn't try to make it look like a company. He didn't have a secretary or anything of the sort. For the most part, it was just him and the higher-ups running the show.

He tried to make everyone feel like we were part of a family and it was working. Everybody here was loyal to him, and I didn't think that that would ever change.

Whoever was on the other side of the door though... I couldn't help but wonder who he was.

"Who is it?" He asked, raising his voice. The environment inside the club was quite packed, music thudding through the walls most of the time. We always got some complaints from the police and the neighbors about that, but they couldn't do much. That was just how we were.

"His name is Cynem Zale. I don't know much about him, just that he's thinking about joining the club."

The president pulled at his beard, saying, "Let him in. I suppose there's no harm in talking."

The fact that he was looking pensive and knew Cynem's name was curious, to say the least. I thought that he didn't know who he was. It looked like I was wrong about that. Maybe Cynem was more important than he appeared to be, which was something that I didn't think I'd ever be saying.

He stepped into the room, smirking as his eyes changed slightly. I knew we didn't like each other much, but I didn't think that he loathed me. Something happened not too long ago and I couldn't put my finger on it.

The president checked him out from bottom to top, scoffing. "A college boy like you, and you think that you can join us? Go back to your mommy, kiddo. Your place isn't here."

"Sir, I'm willing to do anything and everything for the cause. I want to prove that I'm worthy."

The president studied him for a couple more seconds, saying, "Well, I suppose that we can at least try and see if you'd be accepted. I don't think you will, but there's no harm in trying, right, Chains?"

Chains was my nickname in the club. We often used our nicknames when referring to each other, though not all the time. I was still stupefied by what was happening to say anything. For the first few seconds after he made that question, I stayed silent.

Realizing that I was looking like a fool – and especially in front of someone that considered me his nemesis – I cleared my throat and replied, "Whatever you want to do, I'm okay with it. The club is yours, after all." After another moment of silence, I added, "So, are we good?"

The president shook his head, sighing. "We are, but only for the time being. I know you'll change your mind eventually."

I curled up the sides of my lips. I walked through the door, stepped outside the room, and said, "Maybe."

"I know you will," he argued.

I walked out of the club as everyone greeted me and I said the bad news. It didn't matter how much I wanted to downplay it – leaving the club where I spent most of my life was always going to hurt me.

Seconds later, I was back on my bike and looking behind me. The building where the club was located would always remain in my mind and I would always think of it fondly.

From now on, I wasn't a biker anymore. The first thing I did, which I never would in other cases, was to put on a helmet. It felt snug against my head, which was way more than I thought I would ever say about it.

I turned on the engine of the motorcycle and then drove home, impatient about being with my husband again. I was pretty sure that he was already feeling the same way, thinking about the life we were going to have together.

But I was going to be respectful of his schedule and that he needed to study. I just wanted to kiss him again and there was nothing wrong with that.

I parked inside the garage of our house, opened the door, and when I found him seated on the floor crying against his knees, I knew something was wrong.

I didn't know what it was, but my heart was tight and I was going to do everything in my power to get the truth out of him.

I got on one knee, grabbing his shoulders. I was shaking him gently when I asked, "Hey, what happened? Why are you crying?"

He was still crying even after I asked him that question, making me feel more worried about it. I thought he was going to keep ignoring me, but then he lifted his head, his eyes red.

"You lied to me."

I gave him an uncomfortable smile, not knowing where that came from. We just got married the day before. What was he going on about?

"What did I lie to you about?" I asked, hoping that he was going to spit out the answer and not dance around it.

"That you weren't in the war. I know you didn't say anything about it, but I think that's something we should all have known before my father decided to marry me to you."

"I married you because we were made for each other and not for another reason."

Seconds later, he was still staring at me, which was making me feel uncomfortable. Not only that, but he was also making me feel that this was unfair. I never thought that my background in the war was important.

It happened so long ago and I wasn't in the military anymore, of course. I wasn't even a biker any longer. I was a person like any other, trying to build a life with my husband.

"But is it true? That you were in the war?"

"Who told you about it?" I asked, helping him stand up. Now that our eyes were almost level, I could feel that I had better control of what was happening. Still, I didn't like where this was going.

"Cynem..." He replied after what felt like an eternity, making me feel as if he just punched me in the gut. I knew something was up when Cynem showed up all of a sudden at the club. I never thought he would. I thought he was just a college student like any other. "He told me everything. He came here after you left."

"I knew he was up to something," I grumbled, punching the air. "And now it looks like he's going to become a biker. He's going to become a member of the Wolf Bikers."

"He told me about that, too. He also told me something else. He said that you killed his parents, and he wants revenge."

I narrowed my eyes, finding that unbelievable. "I was in the war. I did horrible things for the government, but I never killed his parents. Even if by some miracle that happened, I couldn't have known. I doubt that they were innocent, anyway."

A moment of unnerving silence impregnated the room, making me feel that Nefion was going to say the unthinkable. Moments later, he threw his arms around me and hugged me tightly.

Seeing that, I put one arm around him and murmured into his ear, "I'm sorry about everything that happened, but I never killed his parents. I refuse to believe someone thinks I did that. I'm going to talk to him face-to-face when I can and I'll clear everything up. I promise you that."

Nefion looked up, finding my eyes.

"I trust you."

And having his trust was more important than pretty much everything else that happened today. It meant that our wedding was still in good standing and that I didn't lose his love.

Regardless, I felt like what we had between us already had a crack in it.

CHAPTER 10

Nefion

The room was dark and I couldn't stay inside of it much longer. The reason for that was pretty simple. I couldn't stay in my husband's house for another minute. Cynem managed to become a biker, and I didn't know how that even happened. All I knew was that he pulled it off and I kept thinking that something terrible was going to come out of that.

I tried contacting him, but he didn't want to pick up the calls. My phone was turned on and I couldn't stand the spread of misinformation and fake news anymore. It was flying from the mouth of one person and then reaching pretty much everyone in the city, and that was saying something, considering that it wasn't very small.

People were saying that Palio was a murderer and that he'd been lying about that this whole time. I couldn't keep going like this, thinking that everything would sort out in the end. It wasn't going to and Cynem was planning his attack.

He didn't tell anyone in the biker club, as else they'd already have kicked him out. But he was a capable man and he'd gather enough supporters to go up against Palio. I was certain about that and it was the only thought in my mind right now.

That and one more thing – the fact that the months were passing and my belly was growing huger. I didn't know if Palio was aware of what he did. I mean, he should be, right? I didn't know for sure, but he was still the same lovely guy from before.

I didn't tell my father the news, though I was pretty sure that, by now, he knew something was up.

I turned in the bed slowly, looking at him and realizing that someone like him didn't deserve what was coming for him. Still, I was scared. He worked as one of my father's bodyguards and he was amazing at his job. I couldn't be any prouder of him and, yet, I knew something was wrong.

Nothing worse than questioning myself all the time, though, I thought, pushing his arm off of me, slipping out of the bed, and walking to the bathroom without making much noise. The phone was turned off, put into silent mode, and it wouldn't wake Palio up. Thank goodness. I wouldn't be doing this without knowing that I was going to be okay.

The bathroom was right by the bedroom. I opened the door slowly, stepped inside of it, and lowered my PJ's pants. I had a pregnancy test tube with me. I didn't think I was going to need it per se, but it was still better than waiting and worrying that I might not be right after all.

I did what I had to do with the pregnancy test, shaking it in front of me as I waited for the results. It felt like minutes were passing, even though it was just seconds. The first red line appeared and then the second one, giving me the confirmation I was looking for. Or rather, the one I was trying to avoid.

It was true. I was pregnant with Palio's baby and I didn't know what to do.

As soon as I got the answer I was looking for, I tossed the tube into the toilet and flushed it. I was relieved that Palio would never find out about it, but it still didn't solve my problems.

I didn't know if I wanted to have the baby.

And the reason behind that was that I made a mistake when we had sex and he didn't use protection. The first days after it happened, I was lying to myself.

I kept saying that it wasn't going to happen, that I wasn't pregnant, and that I had a full life ahead of me without having to care for a baby. Now that I was thinking about it, I realized I'd been so stupid. Of course he knocked me up. That was just like him. He liked to lie and use me.

All because he ventured somewhere dangerous and life-threatening to find out if I was his fated mate. After all, every Alpha had an Omega, and apparently I was supposed to be his partner – for the rest of my life.

I was fine with that as long as our married life didn't have to involve anything more complicated than loving and having sex, but I knew he wanted more. It was clear in his eyes how he wanted to build a family with me. He wanted to have not just this baby, but many.

I didn't think I was ready for that, even though I also knew it was already too late. If I said to my Omega father what was going on in my mind, he would slap me around and say how stupid about it I was being. But for him, it had been so much easier. He didn't have to marry a biker, didn't have to choose between his life and having a family, and was able to better choose what he wanted when he was much older.

I opened the door of the bathroom slowly, with my PJ's pants back on, and walked to the outside of the house. When I was in the backyard, I walked over to the swing that we had. I sat on it, started to swing, and then made a call I thought I never would.

I needed help and there was only one person I knew that had been in the same situation I now was.

It was dark, but I knew he was going to look at the number and pick up the call as soon as he saw that it was me.

Minutes later, when I heard his voice, it was like I knew everything was going to be much better.

"Bren, it's so good to hear your voice. I'm so sorry I'm calling you in the middle of the night. It's just that... Something terrible is happening to me and I don't have anyone I can talk to."

"Nefion? Oh no, it's okay. You can talk about whatever it is that's bothering you."

I checked what was around me, feeling a little paranoid. I felt like Palio would jump out of the shadows and confront me about the call. Thankfully, it looked like that wasn't going to happen.

"I think I'm pregnant." I tsked, feeling impatient. "Scratch that. I *know* I'm pregnant and I don't think I'm ready for that. Can I stay at your place? It's the only place where I know I'll be safe until I can figure out what to do."

"Of course you can stay here for as long as you want, but what's really going on? You've always said that you were happy with Palio."

"I'm just scared. I don't want to have a baby."

"That's understandable, but you should have talked to him about it before it happened. Now, it might be a little late for that. How long has it already been since it happened?"

"I think... A couple of months. It's been difficult to keep track of time. I'm focused on college and figuring out my life. That's one of the reasons why I don't want my life to change so much. I want to develop my professional career and grow as a person."

"Do you think you can have all of that even though you would have to care for him?"

"I don't know. All I know is that I feel suffocated. I need time to think and a better place to stay."

I heard a deep, audible sigh coming from the other end of the call.

"That's okay. I know what you're going through. Just come to my house as soon as you can."

"Can it be tonight? I don't know if I can spend another day here. I know it will hurt him, but I plan on figuring out everything before it's too late. I'm such a stupid kid."

"You aren't a kid anymore and you need to grow up."

"You're right. Thank you for being my friend."

CHAPTER 11

Palio

I dropped my arm over the other side of the bed, hoping to find my mate, but it was empty. I didn't feel anything, didn't feel anyone, and my heart was soon pounding and racing. My eyes shot open. Something was wrong and I didn't know what it was. He was always by my side when I woke up.

The first thought that popped up in my mind was that he'd gone to the kitchen to make breakfast. I sat up on the bed, looking from side to side.

If that was the case, then the smell of bacon should already be floating in the air, but that wasn't what I was feeling right now. If anything, I couldn't smell anything and could feel like there was an emptiness in my heart.

I shoved the comforter over to the other side of the bed, jumped out, and rushed over to the kitchen. I was always obsessed and desperate when it came to Nefion.

It wasn't that I thought someone would try to harm him, but I was so deeply in love with him that I needed, all the time, to know where he was and what he was doing. I was just finding it so weird that he'd disappeared all of a sudden without telling me anything about it.

I went to the other rooms of the house, including the bathroom and the living room, but I didn't find him. I looked outside and noticed that my motorcycle was still on the driveway. He didn't take it to go anywhere, that much was certain.

Still, I couldn't help but feel that something happened at night, and I couldn't put my finger on it. I jumped back into the house, snatched my phone, and dialed his number. I thought that I was going to hear his phone ringing in the house, but it wasn't. It was calling him, but he wasn't picking it up.

I was more desperate now than I'd ever been in my life and that was saying something. I'd gone through so much.

"Fuck," I barked, hurling the phone against the wall and hearing the screen cracking. I didn't feel bad about that. The phone didn't matter right now. What mattered was finding out what happened to my Omega and why he wasn't in the house all of a sudden.

Could I think that maybe he went out to buy something? No, I didn't think so. Not only did we live in a neighborhood where we couldn't have commercial buildings nearby, he never went out without first telling me about it, and certainly not in the middle of the night.

No. Something was up and I needed to know what it was.

Just when I was crossing the living room, I heard the sound of a motorcycle pulling over. At first, I didn't think much of it. It could be anything. Maybe someone from the club was looking to make small talk with me or something like that. It wouldn't be the first time it happened.

Nevertheless, I needed to go to the window to find out what was going on.

I went there, opened it, and wasn't surprised when I saw Cynem getting off his bike. He took off his helmet and leered at me, a mischievous smile appearing on his face.

"Looks like I just found what I came here looking for," he growled, his voice getting thicker.

"I don't have time for you," I said, shutting the window and going to my bedroom. I put my clothes back on and even my biker jacket, which was an item that I hadn't used since getting out of the club. It made me feel calmer.

I had a plan. I was going to get on my motorcycle and go to the club. The president was still one of my friends and he would understand what was happening. He would offer his help, which was everything I needed.

The first suspicion I had over what happened was that someone had kidnapped Nefion. I didn't see any indications that that was the case, but it wasn't that he disappeared without telling me anything. I didn't see any signs that one of the doors or one of the windows was forced, but I wasn't going to wait until my mind figured out everything on its own.

All that mattered was that the possibility was there. I needed to clear that up before it was too late.

I was just crossing the doorway out of the bedroom when my eyes caught sight of something small and white on the side table. At first, I didn't think much of it. It was probably just a small piece of paper left by Nefion or me that we forgot about, but then I decided to take a closer look.

It was addressed to me, and my heart was already pounding harder again.

Since it was addressed to me, then most likely it was regarding his disappearance. My mind didn't even want to consider the possibility, but Nefion might have walked out on his own, which hurt me.

After all, even though we didn't have much money, I was still doing everything in my power to help him. I was always doing everything I could to show him how important our love was.

I picked up the small piece of paper, unfolding it as I started to read what it said.

My mind was so focused on it that it didn't even register that Cynem just kicked the front door open.

Hey, it's me, your beloved husband. I'm so sorry I have to write this letter to you, but I really don't see another way out of this. I'm leaving tonight. I'm not going to tell you where I'm going, but you need to know that you won't be seeing me for quite some time.

The thing is that... I'm pregnant and I'm sure that the baby is yours. It's all so overwhelming that I don't want to even think about it for now. I know I'm probably being unfair about the whole thing, but I just need to be with someone that was once in a very similar situation.

I need to think things through. I think... I really love you and I want to make our baby happy as well, but I need to understand what's really going on in my mind and how I feel about everything. My life is changing so much, which is something I never thought about when we were still planning the wedding.

Don't come looking for me. I'll be back when I'm ready, if you are okay with that.

Nefion

I was still holding the piece of paper in my hand, and my whole body was trembling. I couldn't believe that the worst nightmare of my life was happening right in front of my eyes. I put the piece of paper back down on the table and turned around when I felt something heavy hitting my face.

I fell over on my back, shooting my eyes open as I tried to piece together what just happened. And then I saw him. Cynem. He was a couple of feet across from me, looming in front of me.

"Where's Nefion?" He barked, his whole body changing. He was becoming more wolflike, and the look in his eyes told me that he was thinking of just one thing – having his revenge. He couldn't accept that Nefion married me instead.

I jumped back up to my feet and assumed a fighting stance. Cynem lunged at me, swinging his arm. I dodged it at the last second and kicked him in his abdomen with my knee. He didn't even flinch, throwing his fist against my face again.

This time, I grabbed it. I squeezed his fist until it hurt him. His body crumbled slightly, but he wasn't one to give up in the first moments of a fistfight. He pressed his foot against my belly and launched himself up, doing a backflip.

I never thought that he'd learn how to fight.

He landed on the floor heavily as his fur started to show and his canines grew bigger. I was holding back. I didn't want to transform right now. I didn't want to kill this guy, no matter how much of a threat he was.

I dodged out of the way when he lunged again, landing with a thud on the floor. Scrambling back to my feet, I let out all the air in my lungs when I found him slamming me against the floor.

My blood was cold until now, but he was forcing my hand and I needed to transform until it was too late. And so I did, letting my claws come out and slashing at his chest. He shrieked when he felt his skin opening. I pressed my foot against him and threw him across the room with enough force to make his body thud against the closet.

Cynem hit his head against the hardwood and fell down on the floor, his head hanging from one side. I stood up slowly, wondering if he was going to get back up. But the seconds passed and nothing happened, and I had more pressing matters to tend to.

I went to the bed, looked underneath it with my hand, and snatched what I was looking for. My shotgun. It would come in handy if someone else was also looking out to kill me.

I picked up my phone as I got on Destiny. Time to tell the president what happened and why I was going to need his help.

CHAPTER 12

Nefion

"So, you really left him because you thought you weren't ready for it?" Bren asked, looking at me with judging and kind eyes. He was supporting me. It didn't matter what he thought was going on in my mind when everything went downhill. He was going to support me all the way, which made me realize that, at the end of the day, he was my only friend.

"I just felt so overwhelmed by it all," I replied, wishing things were different. I wished that I was okay with the pregnancy and the fact that I was going to be a father.

I wasn't going to lie. Even though I thought I wasn't sure about it in the beginning, the months that I spent with Palio were more than enough to change my mind. I loved him. It was something I thought I would never say about anyone. Love wasn't something I could control.

I kept saying to myself that I was going to focus on my career and how important college was to me, but I realized that those things didn't matter as much. What mattered was making sure that I was happy with myself and my life.

Now that a couple days had already passed since I left our house, I couldn't help but feel that I made another mistake. It was one thing walking out of the house and leaving him behind, and another to be living away from him and without all the comfort he could give me.

Bren put his hand on mine, caressing it.

"I went through something similar. I'm Cogwyn's fated mate, as you know. The biggest difference is that he also never believed in it. We had to run away from the Bear Bikers in our city. He was all the way with me, always protecting me. Palio's been doing something similar for you, hasn't he?"

His question was genuine, and he was right about that, too.

I looked down, feeling shame overwhelming my heart. I couldn't control it. I just kept making one bad decision after the other, even though I realized I wouldn't have come to that conclusion if I wasn't here.

"Maybe I should talk to him again. Do you think he will forgive me?" I asked, looking at his eyes and finding the same kindness from before.

He nodded slowly, grabbing my hand and standing up with me.

"I did even worse things to Cogwyn and we're still together, as you can see."

As he finished saying that, Cogwyn appeared from behind him and wrapped his arms around his chest, kissing the nape of his neck. It was so reminiscent of the mornings and the nights I had with my husband, who I was very sure was desperate and searching for me.

"You're going to be okay. If you need my help, I'll be there to help you," Cogwyn promised, making me feel so happy that I had their support, no matter what happened. It was so great to know that I had true friends that cared about me. They were so different from the assholes that always wanted to hang out with me, but were never available when I needed them.

I rubbed my hands over my face as I tried to make my mind about it.

There was no denying it. I needed to go see my husband and

tell him about everything that happened.

I turned, announcing the news to Bren and Cogwyn when I heard the engine of a motorcycle in the distance. For the first few seconds, I didn't think much of it. Some motorcycles were very loud and we were relatively close to a very busy freeway. Sometimes, we could hear motorcycles riding on it.

But then I noticed that something was different about that engine. I knew that sound. I knew it like the back of my hand.

It was Palio's motorcycle, Destiny. I could still remember how I felt when I first got on it.

Out of the trees and shrubs he came, riding on the motorcycle and pulling up by the front of Bren's house. He had his helmet on, which was something he was still working on. He said that it was just his custom. He didn't like wearing helmets, and I convinced him about the importance of putting them on.

Even though it was a surprise that he found out I was here, I was worried. I thought he was going to flip out at me. There was a good chance he might. After all, I abandoned him without telling him anything about the truth. I hid the truth from him and he should be angry at me, even though I knew he wasn't going to be.

"Nefion, why did you do this?" He asked, throwing his arms around me after rushing over, ignoring the couple behind me. He hugged me so tightly I felt all the air going out of my lungs.

I missed this. I never thought that I would be saying this, but I missed being hugged by my husband and it was so splendid that he was here. I thought I was going to have to go back to our house and do this without the support of Bren and Cogwyn, and I was happy that things were happening differently.

My face still buried on his chest, I said, "I'm so sorry. I was so overwhelmed by it all."

He put his hands on my shoulders, pushing me so that I was looking at his face. His eyes were watery. He was crying, which was something I never thought I would be seeing him doing one day.

"What happened? Did someone kidnap you? Did these people hurt you?" He said, throwing his finger at Cogwyn. "If they did, I don't know what I'll do, but it won't be nice."

I stepped to stand between him and Cogwyn and Bren, shaking my hands in front of me. "It's nothing like that." I turned my head to look at them, opening a very weak smile on my face.

"They helped me. I needed somewhere to stay for a couple days until I figured out what I wanted, and they were willing to host me. I even cared for their baby once when I was younger."

It was cold here, as it always was. The place was covered in snow. Everything was white and so beautiful, too. I never said this to Palio, but one of the things I wanted to do was to live in a very similar place. Did I think it could be made real? I didn't know, but I could bring that up to Palio.

His expression softened up when he realized that I wasn't lying.

He lowered his eyes before locking them with mine. "You should've told me about this. You should've told me everything. You should never hide anything from me."

I wrung my hands. "I know. There's just something important I need to tell you."

"And you should keep your ears perked up for it. It's the biggest news of your life," Cogwyn said, still hugging his husband from behind. They were like the perfect couple and I wanted to be more like them. Everything was becoming much clearer to my eyes. I wanted to be like them because it was what would make me happy.

I grabbed his hand, feeling how big and heavy it was. My hand was tiny in comparison.

"I told you about it in the letter. I'm not sure if I made it pretty clear, but I really am pregnant and I know that the baby is yours. I didn't even plan for it, which is one of the biggest reasons why I left you. It was overwhelming. My whole life was going to change and I didn't know how to deal with it."

He hugged me tightly again, burying his face in the crook of my neck.

"I'm so happy for you and us. It's good that you're telling me this in person. When I read your letter, I didn't believe it."

And now I realized that I wanted to be together with him for the rest of my life.

CHAPTER 13

Palio

I opened the door of the house, wondering if I was going to find that asshole still around here. I checked out the living room, then the bathroom and the kitchen and the bedroom, not finding him anywhere. Feeling a little relieved, I was pretty sure that that hadn't been the last time I saw him. Cynem would show up again eventually and when he did, I'd be ready for him.

I already told the president about what happened. He'd sort things out. The guy was on the run, but with all of the Wolf Bikers gunning for him, he wasn't going to last much longer. I was sure about that and was salivating.

I closed the door of the bedroom, pushing Nefion against the wall. He moaned softly, locking his eyes with me as he asked, "What were you looking for when you opened the door? It almost looked like you were hunting for something."

"Cynem. He was here looking for a fight. I knocked him out cold and then went out searching for you."

"Cynem..." He looked down, sounding almost sad about it. "I don't know what happened to him, but he lost his way. I never thought that he'd be one to pick a fight."

"Well, he won't survive much longer out there. The Wolf Bikers are looking for him and they'll sniff him out. When that happens... I don't like thinking about it, but they don't treat traitors kindly. He should never have tried to kill me. The president and the rest of the club will never forgive him."

After a moment of silence, Nefion asked, "Can you do a favor for me?"

I smiled, knowing that he was pregnant and that I couldn't do anything he didn't want. After all, I'd do anything to make sure the baby was happy, and it didn't matter the cost of that. Nothing and no one would stand in our way.

"Ask the pack not to hurt him. I want to talk to him in person and show him that he really can't have me anymore. I know why he's acting like this and doing these things. He's so in love with me that he can't stop thinking about me, and that's something I can relate with."

I groaned, the first thought that came into my mind that I should really do that. After all, I needed to make sure that Nefion thought I was always on his side, no matter what.

I lifted his chin, saying, "Fine. I'll do it."

"And tell them that keeping him alive is the most important thing they can do. I don't want them to hurt or kill him, and it's not about how I feel about it, even though I would never forgive myself if they did that. I know he has a good heart."

"Fine. I promise, dear," I murmured, sealing our lips again and rubbing them together, making him moan. Pressing his body against the wall, I couldn't help but lift his shirt and take it off.

After spending days without my husband, there were a lot of things I wanted to do with him and this was just one of them.

He parted his lips, allowing my tongue into his mouth. I battled against his tongue for a little while, winning control over the fight seconds later. Nefion was melting in my arms and I was loving the way he was doing that. As an Omega, he was so submissive.

Our kiss was very passionate and slow, and I could keep on kissing him for hours on end. It did feel like hours were passing even though it was just seconds.

When he pulled his head back, he was breathless. His eyes were locked with mine and he was telling me so many things through them.

His hands roamed over my body, going down and finding my belt. He smiled without showing his teeth as he undid it and took it off. It fell to the floor, my dick hard and raging. I wanted to be inside of him. I wanted to knot my Omega, and I was pretty sure he was thinking the same.

When he regained his composure and was breathing more normally, he got on his knees and lowered my pair of briefs. The look in his eyes was telling me everything. He was loving what he was seeing. My dick was hard and pointing at him, pre-come seeping out of the slit.

He didn't say it, but the look on his face was more than telling. He missed my cock.

He looped his fingers around it slowly, as if he was afraid of what might happen. He started to pump my cock over and over. When he had his fill of that, he started to play with my balls, loving how warm they were.

I took a step toward him, sliding my cock between his lips. They were very warm and welcoming, and I couldn't see myself doing anything different. For a moment, I really thought I had lost him, but now I realized it was nothing more than a bad dream and that it would never happen again.

I grabbed his hair and started to move his head up and down along my cock, loving the way he was deep-throating me without gagging. He learned so much about sex it was impressive. I taught him so much and now I was reaping the benefits.

He pulled back, kissing the tip of my cockhead when he had his fill of it, too.

His lips were wet and covered with my pre-come, and he wasn't ashamed of that. If anything, he was proud of it.

Nefion then stood up, kissed me again, his hand roaming

over my body as he took off my leather jacket. I let him do it. He needed to feel more of me and he was going to get everything he craved. Our bodies were so hot we were already sweating, even though it was cold outside and we could already see snowflakes falling from the sky.

This afternoon was perfect for what we were doing, the sun falling behind the houses and casting different shades of orange and gold.

I snuck my fingers under my white shirt, lifting it up and over my head. I tossed it to the side, where it couldn't bother us. As soon as Nefion's eyes danced over what his mind had been thinking about this whole time, he took a deep breath.

He didn't need to say it, but he loved my chest. It was built like a tank, covered by scars and tattoos. He moved his right hand over it, stopping at my nipple before he said, "This almost feels like a dream. I'm so glad it is not."

"No, it really isn't," I murmured, scratching his chin and pecking his lips again, feeling so hard right now it was almost impossible to not just bend him over and fuck him until I was knotting him.

I could feel my eyes changing, my wolf side wanting to come out. It wasn't going to. I was keeping it at bay.

He twisted my right nipple and then dove his head, wrapping his lips around it. I groaned, closing my eyes and putting both of my hands on the back of his head. I kept it where I wanted it, his lips working my nipples as his hand continued to jack me off.

Gosh, I missed this so much.

My breathing was quickening when he went for my other nipple, his hand going up and down along my dick, pulling at the skin. I was doing everything in my power not to come right now. I'd only do that when I was inside of him and murmuring that he was the love of my life.

Seconds later, he pulled his head back again and kissed me one more time, grabbing my hand and leading me into our bedroom.

He pushed me down against the bed and laid me on it. I spread my arms around him, pulled him to me, and made out with him for what felt like an eternity, flipping around when the time was right for the thing I'd been most waiting for.

Knotting him again.

I took off the rest of his clothes in a hurry, tossing them over my head. I didn't need to glance down at his butt to know that he was wet and already waiting for me.

I curled up the side of my lips slightly, lining up my shaft to his orifice and breaking in. When I was inside of him, I started to roll my hips and grew bigger as my orgasm surged. I was knotting him, coming inside his tunnel for what felt like an eternity.

I pulled out moments later, falling onto the bed heavily and bringing him to me with my arms. I kissed the side of his neck, cocooning him in arms before murmuring into his ears, "You're the most important person in the world for me. Don't you ever forget that."

"I won't," he replied gently before closing his eyes and falling asleep with me.

While I couldn't sleep and feel rested right now – there was still the matter of Cynem to resolve – we could spend the rest of the day and the night together, not thinking about anything that didn't involve only us.

And then, tomorrow morning, we'd settle the score with Cynem.

CHAPTER 14

Cynem

I cracked my eyes open, realizing that nothing changed since yesterday. I was still with my lover and, this time, he was by my side. I could hear his soft snoring and it was very relieving. He was with me. He didn't flee from me like last time and would never try the same again.

I groaned gently, pushing myself off the bed as I put on a pair of trousers. I looked behind me to make sure that my Omega was still sleeping, and I smiled when I realized he was. He was with his arm hanging from the bed, drooling from one of the sides of his mouth.

Satisfied with what I was seeing, I went to the kitchen and started preparing something nice for him. I knew that this morning he was going to wake up with his belly hungry and begging for food. We had been living long enough for me to know what his food tastes were like, and I was keeping that in mind as I turned on the flames of the stove.

I opened the open, grabbed the pots and pans I was going to need, and then went to the fridge. I popped the door open, took all the other things I was going to need, and then went to the kitchen island. I was going to make bacon, eggs, pancakes, and a lot of other things for my beloved.

My Omega was going to be so hungry he was going to eat all

that and a lot more, too. Thinking that, I was keeping in mind that I needed to excel this time. I needed to be better than my usual self and make the best homemade breakfast he ever had.

I was in front of the stove and dealing with the pans when I heard footsteps approaching the kitchen. It could only be one person, so I was already opening my smile when I saw that it was him. Nefion was in the doorway, supporting his weight against it.

He rubbed the sides of his eyes before saying, "Good morning! It smells very nice what you are making."

I adjusted my apron, going to him after rounding the kitchen island. I wrapped my arms around him, kissed him again, and then looked at his eyes. Even though he was kind of sleepy, he was showing me how happy he was with the way things turned out.

"Hungry?" I asked, pulling one of the chairs so that he could sit on it. He had to put on his clothes before coming to the kitchen as did I before starting to make the breakfast proper. Even though it was nice to be naked inside my own house whenever I wanted, there were times when I needed to do things – like making breakfast – which required my full attention.

I wasn't a cook and I sure as hell wasn't good at cooking, but I was making an exception for my fated Omega.

"Yes. I'm so fucking hungry," he replied, giving me the confirmation I was looking for. I was pretty sure that it didn't matter if I fucked up or not, he was going to love the breakfast I was finishing regardless.

I smiled, went back to the stove, turned off the flames, and then prepared a plate for him. After putting the cutlery he was going to need, he grabbed them and dug in, smiling without showing his teeth.

I was a little nervous. It wasn't the first time he was eating something I whipped up, but it didn't matter. My heart was always tight whenever he was eating something I made.

Wringing my hands, he took another bite of the bacon and eggs, widening his soft smile.

"It's very delicious. Thank you for this. Thank you for being with me, even though I know I fucked up."

I went behind him, settled my hands on his shoulders, and kissed his cheek.

"Don't worry about it. I know you did it thinking about what was best for me and you. I don't hold it against you."

"I'm so lucky to have you," he said and we kept chatting until we both finished our breakfasts. I did the dishes, dried my hands, and then went with him to our bedroom. He was opening his backpack when I hugged him from behind, pressing my groin against his ass.

"I missed you so much. Could you not go to college today?" I asked, hoping that he was going to concede. "I know I'm being selfish, but it's the way I am. I'm jealous. I'm obsessed with you and want to make sure that you are happy. I can only do that when you are with me."

Nefion turned around in my arms, putting his hands on my waist.

"I'm going to think about that. I can't make any promises, though."

"Now you're just teasing me."

He pressed his finger against his lips and then lowered his hand, smiling gently.

"Fine. I won't do that, but we need to do something else to fill up the time. We had breakfast and it was really delicious. Now we need to have something equally tasty."

I studied his eyes, reading what he was thinking.

When Nefion was in the mood, it was impossible not to do what he wanted.

"And what's that?" I purred, moving against his body and feeling how small he was. I thought that this morning we weren't going to do anything sexy, but I realized I was wrong about that. My body was begging for this.

"You know what I'm talking about."

And I did. I didn't need him to say anything else. I just dove in, sealing our lips one more time. We were kissing again and just like all the other times, there was something different about it. Every time we made out, we understood each other better.

We broke the kiss with a plop, his lips refusing to disconnect from mine.

Just like all the other times, he was breathless and I knew he needed more. An Omega like him would never be satisfied with just one kiss, and I was sure he was thinking the same way.

I moved my hand down, cupping his bulge as I started to massage it. He groaned, lying down on the bed as I started to lower his pants. Then, I got rid of his pair of boxer briefs and was all over his shaft.

As a morning gift, I was going to make him come in my mouth.

Without a second thought, I got on my knees and put my fingers around his cock. Not as big as mine, but this wasn't about his size. It was all about bringing him as much pleasure as he could feel, and it was working.

Sliding my hand up and down over his shaft, I worked it, making it a little harder than it was. His cockhead was bulbous and purple-ish, pre-come leaking out of it.

I couldn't help but stick my tongue out and lap it up, his body shaking in pleasure. When I had my fill of that, I kissed the tip of his dickhead – just like he did for me that time – and then sides of his shaft, loving its girth and length.

Gosh, I could spend all day doing this.

Satisfied with that, I snuck one of his balls into my mouth and started to apply pressure on it. Swirling my tongue around it, I felt his body growing hotter, the need to orgasm becoming clearer.

He tilted his head backward and shut his eyes. As I put his

other nut inside my mouth and kneaded his legs, he let out a groan of lust as his dick finally erupted. I tightened my lips around it and locked it where it was, shooting rope after rope of his milk all over my mouth.

I smiled, moving away from it and then lying on the bed with him. His dick was getting softer again and I was sure that he was already planning on what we were going to do tonight.

I had to spend so many days without him that my wish now was to make sex with him all the time, no matter how tired we were.

NEFION'S EPILOGUE

When I woke up, I realized that my husband was already seated on the bed. I thought that it was already nighttime and he was going to prepare dinner for us, but then I realized the sun was still high in the sky and that the light coming through the windows was very bright.

We didn't sleep per se. We only took a very short nap and I wondered why. I always slept a lot when I was okay with everything that was going on in my life. It should be the case now that I made up my mind and decided I wanted to continue being married to him.

I opened and closed my eyes, noticing that he was holding his phone to his ear. He was talking to someone and it looked pretty important. Not only that, but his shoulders looked so tense I was pretty sure it was more than that. He was worried about something.

"I'm on my way," he stated, ending the call and putting his phone back down on the nightstand. I thought he was going to notice that I was already awake, but he didn't. During the next few seconds, he didn't say anything, staring at the closet like something was going to jump out of it.

I cleared my throat gently and he turned around, smiling when he noticed that it was just me.

"I heard what you said. Did something happen?" I asked, hoping that he wasn't going to dance around the question.

He put his hand on my thigh, saying, "I think I've got big news for you."

"What sort of big news?" I asked. The way he was looking at me was making me worried something was up. He wouldn't be awake now if that wasn't the case.

"They got him."

"They got who?"

"Cynem. He's surrounded and the president wants us to go there to talk to him. I think that he's trying to kill himself."

I bulged my eyes, incapable of wrapping my mind around what he just said. I couldn't believe it. The man that was always so strong, so determined about everything, and always certain of his choices was now trying to kill himself? It didn't make sense. And if it did, I would feel terrible about it.

"What happened to him? How did you manage to catch him?"

He got up, put his clothes back on, and replied, "We need to go there right away. I said I'd do whatever was needed to end the problem we have with him and now is the right opportunity for that. Remember that you said you wanted to talk to him in person, too."

"I know and I'm going to. It's just difficult thinking that this is finally going to happen. After he came here and… Kissed me without my consent, I thought I would never be able to forgive him."

Hearing that, Palio pushed himself away from me, driving his hand over his face.

"I was ready to do the same for him, but please don't tell me he really did that."

Realizing the mistake I just made, I knew there was no going back. My husband wanted to know the whole truth and that was it. It was part of the truth and it couldn't be omitted.

I stepped toward him, putting a hand on his shoulder. He had his back turned to me, like he was doing everything in his power to hide what his face was showing. It wasn't like it was working, though. I could feel how tense his shoulder was. If it were possible, he would snap Cynem's neck, and that was putting it mildly.

"I never told you about it, but it did happen and, for what it's worth, I didn't like it."

He lifted his hand, fisting it.

"It's unforgivable. He knew you were married to me. He crossed a line that should never have been crossed."

"I know you're right and I don't ask for your forgiveness. I just hope you understand. I never thought Cynem was like that too, but he showed that he is someone different. He has some issues he needs to deal with and we need to prove that we are better than him."

He opened his hand, lowering his arm. Turning around so that his eyes were seeing me, he took a deep breath and appeared to be calming down.

"You're probably right, my love," he said, kissing my lips softly and going for his helmet. He picked it up, opened the door of the garage, and I sat down on it.

He helped me put on my helmet, which was such a significant progress for him that I was impressed by it. Little by little, Palio was learning the importance that came with protecting ourselves when he was riding his motorcycle.

He twisted the handlebars and we rode off, arriving at the destination moments later. A crowd was already gathering by the front of the building. When I looked up, I spotted what I was looking for. Cynem and a bunch of other bikers, including the president, standing by the edge of the roof of the building.

He had his gun pointed to his face and was threatening to kill himself if they continued to approach him. I didn't need to be right there with them to know what was going on in his mind.

He wasn't pulling our leg. He wasn't trying to fool us. If the bikers took another step toward him, he would kill himself.

It was just crazy that, this whole time, I never noticed that he had mental issues. I knew he was obsessed with me, that he had an uncontrollable crush on me, but I never thought it was so crippling.

I got off the bike and went to the elevator of the building. Palio was right behind me as I pressed the button to go to the roof. The elevator doors opened and we jumped out, finding ourselves where everyone else was.

As we stepped toward them, the president of the biker club turned his head to look at us. I didn't need to look at his eyes to know what he was thinking. He was confused about everything and wanted to put an end to it his own way. Problem was, I wasn't going to let that happen.

I stepped through the crowd as I found myself a couple of feet in front of Cynem.

"Cynem, what the hell do you think you're doing? You're better than this."

"I was wrong about it."

"About what?" I asked, feeling confused as well.

"About who killed my parents. It wasn't Palio."

I scrunched up my eyebrows. I could grasp what was going on in his mind. This whole time, he put the blame on Palio, but it turned out he didn't have anything to do with it. I was already feeling more relieved. I never forgot about that, but it was good to know it was never a problem.

"You should be happy. You are admitting that you made a mistake."

"But there's a problem with that."

"And what problem is that?" I asked, stepping toward him as I tested the waters. I was wondering if he could really do it. I was almost sure he couldn't kill himself because it was me this time, and it appeared that I was right. He didn't pull the trigger now.

He pointed with his head toward the president, replying, "It was the president. This whole time, I whored myself for him, trying to do everything to please him, and even joined the pack, but I made a mistake. He was only using me. He was the one who killed my parents."

Palio turned his head to look at him, arching his eyebrows.

"Is it true? Were you really in the war?"

The president waved his hand, narrowing his eyes.

"I never told you, but I was. I just thought that it didn't matter. It was such a long time ago."

"You should have told us. Everyone here deserved to know it."

"I suppose you're right. I don't care about it. I just want this shit to be over."

I stepped toward Cynem, grabbed the hand that was holding the pistol, lowered it and then stepped away from the edge of the roof with him.

When it was clear that he wasn't going to kill himself anymore, I heard a collective sigh of relief around me. He was still shedding tears when he lamented, "I don't know what to do anymore. I don't want to be a biker, I don't want to be in college, and nobody loves me."

I didn't know what to do, either, but I couldn't abandon him. Even though it wasn't my responsibility, I was going to find a new goal for his life.

PALIO'S EPILOGUE

I was in the hospital, pacing from side to side in front of the door. Months after what happened on the roof of that building, I could say that I certainly felt much better about what happened. We found a place for Cynem, the guy I couldn't stand.

My progress in terms of feeling empathy was astounding. My whole life, I thought that I only cared about myself and finding my mate. I thought that nobody else mattered to me, but then I realized there was more to life than that.

It was one of the reasons why I was also worried about the fate of my baby. They were still performing the operation and the room was so small, especially for someone my size.

My friends from the biker club were worried about what was going to happen as well. They were with me in the hallway, looking confused and uncomfortable.

They wanted to step up and help me figure things out, but they couldn't. Many of them hadn't found their mates yet, after all.

The president was also here with me, though our friendship was already cracked. What was revealed during the incident a couple of months ago was forever going to remain in my mind. I was sure of that and couldn't stop thinking about it every time I looked at him.

"You should calm down. It's going to be fine, really. This is one of the best hospitals in the city and the doctors and nurses are professionals."

"I know, but it doesn't matter. Nefion needs me right now. He needs me holding his hand, telling him over and over that everything will be alright."

He shrugged, shaking his head. "Well, you know that can't happen. That's what the doctors and nurses said. Not to mention that you take up too much space in the room."

Everyone laughed out loud at that and I even tried to smile, but this was no time for jokes. I was so worried that I felt like my body was wrong and that I shouldn't be in it.

Then, one of the nurses opened the door and announced, "You can come in, but only you."

I looked at everyone that was in the hallway and I was happy when I got their nods of confirmation. I went into the room, pushed past the doctors and the nurses, and went to where my lover was. In his arms was the most beautiful and tiniest thing in the world.

I was already by their side when he said, "I saw you outside so grumpy and worried. That was so you."

I didn't know what to do. I knew that I had always worked toward this moment, but I didn't know what I'd do when it was actually happening. I was a father now and I had a baby. It was a baby boy.

"He's an omega, just like me," Nefion said, almost as if he was reading my mind.

My baby was an Omega? It was like a dream come true. I mean, I'd have been equally happy if he was an alpha, but there was just something different knowing that he was an Omega.

"You look surprised. I mean, he was always either going to be an Alpha or an Omega, or maybe a Beta."

I knew what was going on in his mind. If our baby was a Beta, there would be problems. Betas were looked down on in our society, more so than the Bikers. They were the middle term between an Omega and an Alpha, and they usually didn't mingle with us.

They lived isolated in some of the most violent neighborhoods in the city, where they usually chose the life of becoming a Bear Biker, if they were shifters like me.

I pushed those thoughts out of my mind. They had no place in it right now.

"Do you want to hold him?" Nefion queried, smiling softly.

Knowing that I couldn't say no, I picked up the baby and held him in my arms. I didn't know how I was supposed to hold him properly, if I was doing this right or was hurting him.

"It's okay. You're doing it right. When you get used to it, it will feel like you've been doing it for all of your life," Nefion said, noticing how uncomfortable I looked right now.

The baby was tiny, making me wonder how it was that something like this could grow into a full man.

"Here, do this," Nefion said, rubbing the tip of the little one's nose until he opened his eyes and looked at me. I didn't know if he knew that I was his father, but I liked to think that, deep in his mind, he was already aware of it.

He started to wave his arms in the air, as if he was trying to grab me. I didn't know what to do right now.

"Show him your finger. He's going to love it," Nefion said, doing just that so that I knew how to do it.

After he retracted his hand, I showed the little one our finger and he moved his hands as if he was trying to grab it. I didn't know if he was going to manage to, but he was still moving his hands in such a cute way I couldn't help but blush.

Moments later, when I thought that it was already a lost cause, he managed to latch his hands around my finger and tug at it. He was quite strong, I noticed. I didn't think that someone so tiny could already grip so firmly.

Then, he started to giggle before letting go of my finger.

"Looks like he's already bored of it. Don't worry. He's like that, I think," Nefion said, offering me his arms. He was asking me to give the baby back to him, which I did. When our little one wasn't in my arms anymore, I felt like something important was missing. I wanted to be holding him for all of eternity.

There were going to be plenty of opportunities for that, I reminded myself.

"He's our little Rein," he said, mentioning the name we chose for our little one. It took us a lot of time, but we managed to find a name that stirred some reaction from Rein when he was still in my lover's belly.

"Yes, he is," I said, kissing the side of his cheek, pulling over a chair, and sitting on it. I took his hand, holding it. "And he will have the best life possible. When you're out of college and working, we'll be making more money than we know what to do with it."

He chuckled as one of the nurses approached us. "We need to take Rein to the nursery, if you don't mind," she said and I sighed. I looked at my husband's eyes, giving him the confirmation he was looking for. He wasn't going to be able to see his son for a while, which sucked, but there wasn't much he could do about it.

"I suppose it can't be helped," he said, holding out the baby and giving it to the nurse.

She put it in her arms and said, "Thanks. Don't worry. You'll be given the green light soon and then you'll be able to go home."

"I'll take plenty of pictures," I offered, giggling with him.

His eyes contemplated me and he then put his hand on my cheek, kissing me moments later. It was a short, passionate kiss that sent goosebumps all over my body. The rest of my life was going to be like this? I asked myself, already knowing the answer.

Of course it was going to be.

"I love you so much," I said and we kissed again, knowing that only good things awaited us.

The End

Thank you for reading this story! If you enjoyed it, you can find more in this series:

Tasting the Omega 1: Rock-Hard

Tasting the Omega 2: Reckless Entry

Tasting the Omega 3: Rough in Public

Tasting the Omega 4: So Big It Hurts

Lastly, leave a review if you liked the book. It always helps me so much!

TEASER: OVERWHELMING THE OMEGA

An Omegaverse MPREG Story (Lost Innocence - 1)

"Come on, Justin. It's yours if you want it," he said. His words were almost inaudible, though I didn't know if it was because of me, given the state of my mind, or because he was losing himself as well.

Slowly, but surely, I moved my shaking hand to his cock. It stood hovering above it for a few seconds before I dared to wrap my fingers around it. The moment they were locked around his big man tool, I sensed the thing throb slightly. Moments after, it was already growing in size.

His cock was warm - more so than the ambient air. It was so inviting to touch something so soft and tender. And I as I moved my hand a bit, I was rewarded by his toy growing a little bit. His balls moved when the side of my hand touched the skin of his sac. They went down a couple of inches, indicating the Hugo was getting in the mood.

Even though things had barely started, I moaned. My hand moved up and down on his shaft. I was doing it slowly not to spook myself. I had no idea how big his toy could get. I also had no idea how loose his balls could be.

His shaft was not in a semi-solid state, though it was evident already that it would be too much for me. My fingers were never going to grip the whole thing.

As it continued to grow thicker, my fingers were forced to open up more space for its veiny surface to expand. It had now such a striking girth that my thumb lost its contact with my other fingers.

All the while, I continued to give him a handjob, not caring one bit that fear was still taking hold of me. I wanted to be calm in that situation, but it was simply impossible while my sight was more and more dominated by his growing package.

His shaft was now fully hard. It was so big that I had to blink twice. My poor mind could not grasp that such a thing existed.

"Suck it," he said, and I didn't need another invitation. My head moved down on the same instant, with my heart still pounding out of fear.

The moment I wrapped my lips around his bulbous cockhead, I knew that was what I had been born for. An Omega in heat like me just needed some good dick to worship before starting a day. My job had already started, but who's to say Hugo would not want me to come back, especially if he liked the blowjob?

MPREG SERIES AND MORE

SERIES - PREGNANT FOR HIM

1. Controlled by the Alpha 1: An MPREG Omegaverse Story
2. Controlled by the Alpha 2: An MPREG Omegaverse Story
3. Controlled by the Alpha 3: Dominating the Fertile Omega
4. Controlled by the Alpha 4: An Omega's Tale of Obedience
5. Controlled by the Alpha 5: A Tale of Obedient Submission
6. Controlled by the Alpha 6: Monopolized in Outer Space

SERIES - LOST INNOCENCE

1. Overwhelming the Omega 1: His Little Doll
2. Overwhelming the Omega 2: Brute Entry and Double Teamed
3. Overwhelming the Omega 3: His Tight Backdoor
4. Overwhelming the Omega 4: Stretching his Front Door
5. Overwhelming the Omega 5: Until he Spasms
6. Overwhelming the Omega 6: Naïve and Untouched

ABOUT THE AUTHOR

Steamy MM stories, baby! Michael Levi can't go a day without sitting down and putting into words all the dirty scenes that sprout in his mind. His collection is diverse, but it's gay love only. You won't find anything else on his author page. And if you are looking for something free, check his mailing list. Warning: it can be extra spicy.

When he isn't writing, he's chilling out by the lake close to his house. Nothing better than kicking back with a martini in his hand as he dreams if he'll ever find the man he wants.